Norbie Gets Screwed

STEELTOWN CHRONICLES, Volume 2

Dave Walker

Published by Dave Walker, 2025.

NORBIE GETS SCREWED

First edition. July 23, 2025.

Copyright © 2025 Dave Walker.

ISBN: 978-1069682819

Written by Dave Walker.

Also by Dave Walker

STEELTOWN CHRONICLES
Making Steven Famous
Norbie Gets Screwed
Johnny Goes Loco
Tony Needs Speed

Watch for more at www.davewalkerauthor.com.

For my genius wife Anne, also a writer. Without you, my books would never see the light of day, and for that I'm eternally grateful.

"Your brain can't tell the difference between something you vividly imagine and something you actually experience."

—Tony Robbins, *Awaken the Giant Within*

"We can be heroes for ever and ever

What d'you say?"

—Bowie, "Heroes"

Chapter 1

SATURDAY, JULY 10, 2003, 8:55 a.m.

Other than marrying Morag, today was the next best thing that *should* have happened to me, Norbert Reingruber, proud Hamiltonian and owner of Steel City Comics, also star goalie for the Village Idiots Road Hockey Team, MegaFreak's number one fan, and now, a bonafide comic book writer and illustrator. *Hot diggity dog!*

"Fuzzin' awesome!" I shrieked, as Spiderman swung on a rope over the ComWorld crowd, shot his web, and ensnared three thugs right in front of me. They struggled to escape but Gotham cops whisked them away down the corridor. The convention centre erupted into raucous cheering. I gave the actors a standing ovation. Spiderman landed on a ceiling rafter, spun around, and waved to his fans. *What a performance!* Marvel had really upped their marketing game. *Wait till the guys hear about this!*

I sat back down, but no way could I stop clapping: my Spidey senses were seriously tingling!

Tye Novak, my crack editor at Slacker Comics, had scored me an autograph table at ComWorld. Only minutes ago, he'd phoned me all the way from Brooklyn, New York, telling me that in less than a week Slacker had received more than five hundred orders for my breakthrough comic book *The Steeltown Avenger*, orders from super cool comic book shops in super cool places like New York City, Los Angeles, and even Japan. How fuzzin' amazing was that? I'm saying fuzzin' because I'm trying not to use real swear words.

I was so excited, I was ramming jelly beans into my mouth. Typically, I couldn't stop stroking my beard—*it's **not** an Elf beard, Pappas, it's just a little thin!* Today, my nervous habit was in full swing for darn good reason. I was practically famous, and, as Tye had told me, it was up to *me* to now make myself *totally* famous. I wasn't going to let Tye down, or Morag, or my fans. My emotions were spinning around inside my head like socks in an industrial dryer, and I had a serious case of Jimmy-leg, and sometimes out of nowhere my leg struck the table leg, and it sounded like a cannon going off, and people would turn and look over at me, and I'd say "Sorry", and my cheeks would go all red. My throat was totally parched, even though I'd drunk all the Orange Crush and bottled water Morag had bought me. I truly hoped I'd have a voice left when my fans showed up. It's bad enough I sound super reedy when I speak, but when my throat gets dry I sound like a cat trying to escape a tenor saxophone.

Morag had gone old school, dressed as Daphne from Scooby Doo, and her purple mini-dress really showed off her nice bum, plus she and Daphne have the same orange hair so it was a perfect choice. Didn't every eight-year-old boy imagine Daphne would be his first girlfriend?

My Jimmy-leg whacked the merchandise bag on the floor beneath me. Morag had fast-tracked the booths before the doors opened to the public and scored a bagful of comic books, figurines, and autographs, then ditched them with me before booting back out for more. My wife is so awesome, let me tell you! She wants nothing to do with the limelight. Instead, she's happy to watch from the wings while I "enjoy the ride", even though she co-wrote the darn book! Man, I'm a lucky guy. Trying not to swear was the *least* I owed her. *I don't deserve you, Morag!*

I had a terrible case of monkey brain. But when I get excited, that's what happens. Same thing happens to my friend Donny, the poor *bastardio,* but way worse. I felt like a hyper kid who'd eaten way too much candy, and the candy was the crowd and I was feeding off them and couldn't stop myself, it was that fuzzin' good.

My confidence was super high. I felt super snug and comfortable because I was wearing my rock and roll armour: my purple long-sleeved Zeppelin t-shirt and black leather vest with all my favourite patches sewn on. And I'd already spotted at least five more beauts at the booth across from me. Man, my vest was going to be even *more* awesome!

I straightened out my shirt so it didn't emphasize my gut. Tony Valentini and John Pappas say I look like a wannabe biker with a crazy Gimli beard, but I disagree, and so does Morag; she says I look like Hermie the Dentist Elf. Besides, instead of a motorcycle, I have my orange Vespa.

I was so blown away by the fact that I was sitting beside real, actual comic book writers! On my left was Dan Cohen, the writer of the awesome comic book *Dragon Man,* on my right, Sue Candle, writer of the *Katy Moore* comic books. They were way lesser known than the big comic book stars, like Mark Millar and Grant Morrison, but at least they were more well-known than me. I wasn't well-known at all. *I'm a total fuzzin' nobody in this business,* a voice shouted inside my head. *I shouldn't be here!*

Sweat was beading on my forehead. *I'm not an imposter. I'm not an imposter. I'm not an imposter.* I breathed in deeply, slowly, and exhaled the way Morag had showed me. *You can do this, big guy,* she'd say.

I glanced at Dan and Sue. Come Monday, I vowed to order their books and stock them in my shop. Being new writers, they needed all the help they could get. I would definitely help them. They deserved it!

As much as I wanted to snag their autographs—*Harlan and Tank would be so impressed!*—I was just too darned shy to ask. Mutti says it's because I have the shy gene, passed down from my Uncle Otto. *Thanks, Uncle Otto, you German bast*—! I stopped myself short of swearing. It wasn't easy, but, I'd promised Morag I'd stop. She said I was beginning to sound like sewer-mouth Donny, and there was no way I'd lower myself to his level. Donny had acted fairly normal when he'd first moved back to Hamilton last year, but after the whole Steven Dundee business, not so much.

I'm brutally shy around famous people, not that I know any actual famous people, except for Steven Dundee, who only became famous once Donny Love made him that way in his book, *Making Steven Famous,* and I'm only half-shy around him, as he's almost a close friend.

But everything Donny wrote about Steven was basically a lie, so, in a way, Steven Dundee is a fictional character now. I'm pretty sure that being a fictional character in a self-published book that only sold ten copies doesn't make you famous, unless it sells a million copies, which Donny's book clearly didn't.

Despite my terrible shyness around famous people, I did meet Maurice last year at Irondale Collegiate when he performed as Steven Dundee, although I didn't actually talk to him, so that probably doesn't count. Also, Donny doesn't count in the least, as he's *always* trying to be famous, and always fails miserably, even with his latest over-the-top, marriage-killing stunt. *Poor Allison, I wonder if she even knows about it yet? How could she miss it? How could anyone miss it?*

All this excitement was really drying out my throat so I guzzled an entire can of warm Coke in a single chug. Then I belched, totally not on purpose. "Sorry," I said to Dan and Sue. Sue looked a bit disgusted. I blushed, my head pulsing like a giant field tomato.

Since I'd arrived, I'd been star-struck like an obsessive weirdo. I was blown away when I saw Jack Kirby, the famous author of *Fourth World Omnibus*, and Rick Geary, who'd written *The Saga of the Bloody Benders*, both men strolling by my booth as if they were just your average ComWorld fans. Jack even nodded at me! And my heart had actually skipped a beat! I wanted to tell him and Rick how much I loved their work. Maybe after my session, I'd gather up my courage, track them down, and get their autographs.

Tye Novak's words from our morning conversation rang in my ears. "Five hundred units, Norb, an incredible start! Remember, relationship building is key, so tell them how much you appreciate them liking and supporting your comic book, and explain to them how *The Steeltown Avenger* is the first in a long series, then hit them hard with the free merch and your business card, then offer some kind of draw so you can get their email address and build a mailing list. Okay? Together we'll make *The Steeltown Avenger* number one. A bright future lies ahead, Norbert Reingruber! Godspeed, my sweet friend!"

Tye's words glittered inside my head like *preciousss* in Gollum's palm.

Slacker Comics was a small publishing company in Brooklyn owned by Tye Novak and his business partner and boyfriend, Alex Jolie. They'd discovered Morag and me on ArtBuzz, this cool website that gave unknown comic book writers and illustrators a free forum to post their work. Tye and Alex had green-lighted our partial, and when Morag and I produced the final draft, Tye credited me as the illustrator, and Morag and I as writers. I'd read real good Google reviews about Slacker, and I was over the moon with excitement, but also in a wicked state of disbelief.

They did not make a mistake, you dummy! I kept yelling at myself. *The Steeltown Avenger rocks! So get a grip, man, it's real, deal with it! Enjoy it!*

I kept expecting to wake up and discover this was all a dream. For the first week, I'd pinched myself at least fifty times a day just to make sure it wasn't. Tye and Alex had been so confident in my work they'd wrangled me a booth at ComWorld. Great fellas, for sure, and so over-the-top supportive.

You're not worthy of being published! "Fuzz off," I shouted at the voice. "Nice fuzzin' try bumhead!" A little kid in Spiderman face paint squished up against his mom's leg, freaked out by me. I smiled at him but he was still pretty scared.

Calm down, I told myself. *Morag thinks you're worthy, and she's usually right about everything, especially when it comes to stuff about you.*

To be honest, I've always believed that you make comic books only because you love doing it, and for no other reason. Any other reason is a bumhead's game. And I'm not a bumhead.

But today I was feeling different. Suddenly, I loved the biz and couldn't wait to meet my fans and loved the possibility I just might make a crapload of dough. *See Morag, I didn't say shit. I mean crap. Aw fuzz, whatever.*

With my comic book and collectibles store barely breaking even, I could seriously use the dough. With Morag's help, months after Talbot's owner Doug Lee had retired, I'd rented the space and started Steel Town Comics.

Maybe if my series went big, I'd score enough to slap a down payment on a house so Morag and I could ditch the apartment and start a family and grow them up with all the comforts and security I'd had.

Fact: few writers get rich making comic books. Maybe none. But that didn't stop me from hoping I might. *Imagine Marvel buying the movie rights to our comic series? Offering us world-wide merchandizing deals?*

I imagined Morag and me posing with the cast and crew of our movie, arms slung over each other's shoulders as we stood on the red carpet, cameras flashing as we filed inside Grauman's Chinese Theatre to watch the premier of *The Steeltown Avenger.* It gave me goosebumps just thinking about it.

I would have kept fantasizing, if not for the arrival of Vampirella. She was wearing a couple of pieces of red material, barely covering up her private lady parts, strutting down the aisle in front of me. Then she actually winked at me. My face was burning up and I was desperate to escape her superpowered Sex Gaze. *I can't look at you, Vampirella! No way! I love Morag. I love you, Morag!* Thankfully, another awesome character caught my attention.

"No way!" I shouted. I couldn't help it. "Psylocke!" She was sexy, too, but her purple hair rocked, and she stayed cool. I gave her a thumbs up and she actually returned it.

My confidence soared. "You look totally awesome, man!" I called out. My voice cracked a little at the end there, but I didn't care. *It's the way I am,* I told myself proudly. *It's like my superpower.*

Some of the ComWorld fans gawked at me. To them, I was a cool comic book artist. I waved my thanks at them, feeling more and more like a real celebrity with each passing second.

It was turning out to be a great morning. I flew out from my booth and had my picture taken with HellBoy, Wolverine, and Sailor Moon.

Pretty soon I was waving to everyone that passed by, especially cosplayers. Man, I really respect a great costume.

"Cool!" I called to a Mighty Morphin Power Ranger, and to Mercy and Echo from *Overwatch*, and also to the Punisher, lugging his massive machine gun. Then I clapped. They deserved it! I wished that I had the confidence to dress up, like those guys.

Then, to top it all off, I saw a real live star!

Oh my gawd, it's him! It's really him! "Bill, I mean, Shatner. Live long and prosper, sir!" I gave him the proper Vulcan greeting, hand gesture and all. Shatner shot me a nervous smile and picked up his pace. He muttered something to his handler. But it didn't bother me. I figured he was getting tired of the convention circuit—hey, maybe I would be too, one day! I smiled at him to show him some ComWorld solidarity but he was already gone. He was pretty fast for an older guy!

I swear I saw Jack Black dressed up as Spider Man, slumming the rows of booths, just like any regular shmo. I almost gave him a shout-out, but then I decided I didn't want to be a total goof and blow his cover. I couldn't wait to tell Donny, Tony and John who I'd seen here! I bet they'd be impressed...or not. At least Donny would be.

I really wished my old buds were here to enjoy my success, or at least be here so I could chat with them. That would have made today perfect, even if I wasn't. But none of them had accepted my invite to the convention. Tony had to work, Donny avoided even giving me an excuse, and John had just laughed at me. Tomorrow, I'd regale them with all my stories over a hot cup of Tim Horton's coffee and a box of chocolate dipped donuts, courtesy of yours truly, after our weekly Village Idiots road hockey game. Then they'd be sorry they missed this.

At nine o'clock, there was change in the air! The security guards walked up to the stanchions and unhitched the velvet ropes. The fans thundered up to meet their favourite writers, like me, hopefully.

My confidence was riding its personal rocket into outer space. I gathered up my courage and looked to my left at Dan Cohen. "Good luck, brother! Hope your day rocks hard." I felt kind of bad when I realized that was something Donny would have said, sarcastic-sounding.

He flashed me a peace sign, but it was hard to see his expression behind his frizz-bomb hair and beard. He reminded me of Harry Potter's Hagrid, if Hagrid hadn't been half-giant. I respectfully returned his peace sign. I smiled at Sue, who had flowing blonde hair parted at the side. Perched on the end of her nose, were a pair of black librarian glasses, just like Morag's. *I love you, Morag! I don't love Sue!*

Sue smiled nicely at me. I was halfway through flashing her a peace sign but her lovely smile made me blush so much I stopped. I've always been awkward with women. I don't have any fuzzin' idea how I found the courage to ask Morag out, or how she found the courage to say yes to a dopey fool like me. *I love you, Morag!*

My heart ached for Sue and Dan. No one was lining up to meet them! How could that be? Their books were great! I'd read how fickle and heart-breaking the comic book business could be to writers, and now here I was witnessing it first-hand. I offered Sue a sympathetic smile, but before she met my gaze, I quickly looked away, afraid to see her sadness and disappointment.

Seven fans filed towards me, clutching *The Steeltown Avenger.* Seven! I got goosebumps all over. I couldn't believe it. People actually wanted my autograph! An autograph from a complete nobody named Norb who ran a crappy comic book store in a nowhere placed called The Village on East Hamilton Mountain! *Is this really happening?* I pinched my thigh. I remembered Tye Novak's encouraging words about relationship building. *You can do this, Norbie Reingruber. Think down payment. Think Morag. Think starting a family!*

"Hey dude," the first fan said, "*The Steeltown Avenger* rocks. You're gonna be big, man! This is the best comic since *U.S. Avengers*." He was a tall, skinny man in his forties, in a black Ramones t-shirt. He was paler than Joey Ramone, if that were even humanly possible. His eyes were beady and intelligent, but he didn't look at me when he spoke. He set the book on my table as if he presenting me with a priceless, ancient scroll. "Please sign it, Mr. Reingruber, I'd be so damn honoured."

Mr. Reingruber?

"I'd also be honoured, Mister," I said to the fan, "*really* honoured." My voice had hit the bottom note of a new, higher octave, that's how excited I was.

I'd bought an expensive fine-point marker just for this moment, and was mere inches from signing the front cover of my book, my adrenalin pumping, my hand shaking with nervous excitement, thoughts of stardom sparkling in my monkey brain like bits of sugary cereal, thinking, *We've arrived! We've arrived! I love you Morag! Thanks for helping me make my dreams come true!*

And that's when, out of the blue, someone or something round and black and creepy bowled violently into the Ramones guy, knocking him backwards.

Is that a dwarf? I thought, remotely, as if waking from a foggy dream. *A creepy dwarf?* Half the guy's face was messed up. Fear totally paralyzed me. Sue yelped out loud.

The dwarf whipped open his trench coat and showed me a silver revolver tucked inside his belt. Light glinted off it. The sight of it dropped my jaw.

"I'm here to deliver a message from Shadow." His voice was so deep it made Darth Vader sound like a castrated choir boy.

"What the hell, dude?" the Ramones guy yelled, shoving back in line in front of the creepy guy.

But when he saw the gun, his face went super pale, and when he saw the creepy guy's horrible face, he turned and bolted. Someone at the back of the line yelled, "Hey what's going on up there?"

The creep flicked his gaze behind him and saw security guards bustling towards him from down the corridor. He spun back around and pressed up against the table, leaning toward me.

His breath stank of beef and cigars.

He grinned a row of dull, gold-capped-teeth. In the really horrible half of his face, shadows swam in the sagging skin there, and his googly eye made me think of a festering egg yolk. My stomach turned and my whole body trembled.

"Who the heck are you?" I whispered, somehow. "And what do you want?"

He leapt onto the table, grabbed my collar and pulled me into him with strong, beefy hands that belonged to a man twice his size. He whispered into my ear, in an unholy voice.

"I'm The *Screw.*"

He grabbed my book, flipped to page six, and tapped a panel in the top left-hand corner, then dropped it onto the table in disgust.

"Shadow read your shitty book. He's royally pissed. Remove all your books from every store and eradicate them by Tuesday, nine a.m., or we *eradicate* you and all your loved ones." He leaned closer. "Understand, *Norbie*?"

"My loved ones?" I stammered dopily.

"I basically just said that, ya fat dope."

"Who is Shadow?" I squeaked.

"Ya don't want to know."

I didn't care that The Screw had fat-shamed me. I only cared about the killing part. I glanced down and realized that I was drawing erratic lines on the Ramones guy's comic book. *Not Mutti! This can't be happening! Why is this happening? Was I imagining all of this? Maybe I was dreaming.*

"And no cops, fatso. Or *everyone* dies, *yesterday!*" He slapped his business card down on the table. "Only call with good news." He flung himself off the table and out into the busy aisle. Security chased after him.

"Wow! That was awesome!" the next fan in line said. "That guy was really freakin' creepy. He should win the Cosplay competition today. *Totally* believable!"

I blinked. He shoved his comic book toward me and I signed it, completely numb.

"Are you okay?" Sue asked, her voice shaking.

I nodded dumbly at her.

"He had a gun," she whispered. "Jesus."

We nodded at each other.

"Price of stardom," Dan said. "Attracts all kinds of weirdos." He guffawed good-naturedly.

The next fan in line tabled her comic and stared at me, biting her lip. There was a crazed look in her eyes. "Destinny, with two n's," she said, willing me to pick up my Sharpie.

I felt as if I was watching myself from across the aisle. The Screw nightmare had yo-yoed me out of myself. My mind was free-floating on a cloud of anxiety and fear.

I signed her book and off she went.

I looked down at the business card. It was black, the Screw's phone number stamped on it in gold-lettering. I carefully slid it into the merch bag at my feet. Then I wished I could wash my hands.

I spent the next four hours in a terrible daze, autographing copies of my book. I guzzled water to try and calm my nerves. My bladder was close to bursting, but I was too freaked out to go to the bathroom.

Today was supposed to be awesome. I was supposed to be having wonderful conversations with my fans, but now all I could muster was an occasional vague and slurry thank-you. I felt as if they were all speaking a foreign language. Morag showed up an hour later and stashed more merch under our booth, and I was never so glad to see anyone in my whole life. I knew by the expression on her face that *she* knew I was messed up.

She draped her arm over my shoulders. Concern wrinkled some of the cuteness out of her face as she whispered into my ear. "You're going to town on your beard, Norb. What's wrong, big man?"

"Tell you later," I said, dully. I tried to clear my throat.

She plunked down in the chair beside me and rubbed my back.

Morag told me later that a hundred people had lined up for my autograph but I couldn't remember any of it. What a rip-off. A dream come true and I missed it! That fuzzin' Screw!

I fought the urge to run and call the police, remembering the Screw's threat. Plus, I'd promised Tye Novak I'd autograph books for the full four-hour signing session. I was caught between a rock and a hard place. I'd never felt so impotent in my entire life.

Despite the painful fact that my dream of being a successful writer was crashing all around me, and my hopes of earning enough money to buy a house and start a family, too, I realized, more importantly, that there might not be a family to support or anyone to support them if I didn't meet that evil dwarf's deadline.

How in God's name was I supposed to rip my books out of stores in three days? Was that even possible? How did one do that? *Fuzz!*

A dark depression slogged into my chest. The Screw's voice echoed super loud in my head.

Why had he been jabbing his finger against the panel on page six? And who the heck was this Shadow?

I flipped to page six and studied my creation. The Avenger was facing off against Dr. Derangio and his powerful invention, the Invisiblator. Why was this Shadow guy upset over a made-up villain with a made-up weapon? I mean, invisibility? Totally made-up. *Right?*

With sinking dread, I suddenly realized I was signing autographs for a first comic book in a long series that was now unofficially dead.

Dark depression belly-flopped out of my chest and down into my gut. It dawned on me that I'd become a character straight out of a dark noir comic. It was up to me to do everything in my power to save my family from certain death. The villains were mysterious and scary and—weird. It was fuzzin' depressing.

Morag's eyes widened when she saw the terror eating up my face.

"The Screw's going to kill us," I mouthed.

Morag shook her head. "Babe, what the hell are you talking about?"

I held up The Screw's business card. "Kill," I said, robotically.

"Norbie, you're stressed out. You haven't been sleeping well. You're imagining things." She snorted. "It wouldn't be the first time, bucko." She looked at my face. "You *are* pale. When they close the line, let's get you a bite to eat. We need lunch. I saw a booth selling corn dogs—your fav!"

Not even the thought of a delicious corn dog could fix me. I went back to numbly signing autographs, using my right hand to steady my left. My signatures looked like Donny's when he was impatient and in a hurry, which was most of the time. The look of sheer terror on my face had niggled Morag that maybe her husband was actually telling the truth and hadn't imagined The Screw. I'd never lied to Morag. I only ever held back the truth for awhile, and she knew that about me, so now I could tell she *half-believed* me.

She bit her lip, her eyes narrowing, as she tried to decide what was wrong with me this time. Suddenly, she looked ten years older. And I knew, straight up, it was *all* my fault because of my stupid comic book.

Stupid Steeltown Avenger.

Chapter 2

IT WAS TIME FOR SATURDAY night dinner at 47 Steel Street. It was a family tradition, and Mutti would never take no for an answer.

Inside my childhood home, I called my mom Mutti; outside, Mom. I figured that one out in kindergarten, after my new friend Donny overheard me and said it sounded like "Mooo-ti", like the sound a cow makes. He thought that was pretty darn funny. So, yeah, I stopped using the German term anytime we were out, and especially at school. I think my Mutti was a little hurt by it, thinking back now.

We'd come over straight from ComWorld. I hadn't enjoyed the rest of the day, at all. Not even the Stargate SG-1 panel with Richard Dean Anderson could cheer me up.

Tonight, for the first time ever, I wished Morag and I hadn't come here for our weekly dinner. I needed to be back at our apartment, uninterrupted, with time to think of a plan to rip my books off of shelves by Tuesday. The Screw kept pinwheeling in my mind. I could hardly focus. How dare he threaten my family! I thought, anger zapping me. *What a fuzzin' bumhead!*

"You don't look well, Norbie," Mutti said, as she set a large plate of crab cakes in the centre of the dining room table. There was a dish of sautéed corn and bell peppers, and a wooden bowl overflowing with fresh garden salad. Steam poured off a bowl of herb roasted potatoes like fresh gun smoke. Mutti attended a weekly cooking class and was always trying new recipes, and tonight was no exception.

Despite my mood, the food looked really good to me, and it got me licking my lips. On the way over on the bus, I'd told Morag everything, and it had made me feel a bit better, like it always did to share with her. So now, some of my appetite actually returned, not-so-shockingly.

"Something's very wrong, Norbert, I can tell." Mutti glanced at Morag, then back to me, her brow furrowing.

My Mutti is Anna Reingruber, and she's seventy-nine. She looks way younger, though, due to her daily regimen of sit-ups, deadlifts, and long walks. She still has her thick German accent, and she has these beautiful large dimples—that's where I get them from. I've always felt she has an angel's face.

Her brown hair is curly, with not a single strand of grey, and when she's happy there's a twinkle in her blue eyes. But if she's worrying, which is often, the twinkle quickly dies.

"I like your red pants," said Karl, raising an eyebrow at me.

"Thanks Karl," I said. "I guess."

Mutti was sitting beside her latest boyfriend, Karl "The Great" Dabrowski, a semi-retired magician she'd met through a dating site called *Sexy Seniors*. I blamed myself. When I moved out, I left my old PC behind, and Mutti taught herself a few computer basics. I wasn't sure what to make of Karl, but he was definitely a big improvement over Mutti's last boyfriend, who she'd also met through the dating site.

On the bus ride over, I'd spilled coffee all over my jeans. At Mutti's, Morag had passed me her red yoga pants from her shoulder bag. You wouldn't believe what you can find in that purse. Mutti had put my jeans in the wash.

I felt like an idiot in those red tights, but Morag reminded me that Superman wore tights, so then I felt a bit better.

"Don't worry about me, Mutti," I said, finally. "Just flustered from a busy day at ComWorld. Sorry if I'm a little distracted."

I caught the look in Morag's eye and realized we were both thinking the same thing—we should have cancelled and stayed home, so we could cook up a plan to save everyone, but Morag was an excellent daughter-in-law and hated to disappoint Mutti.

Morag pressed a smile on her face and sighed.

"Well, a good dinner will make you feel better, Norbie," Mutti said, sounding happy. "Everybody dig in before it gets cold."

Karl smiled at us with a top row of perfectly white teeth. The bottom ones were more like grey tombstones pocked by acid rain. Before Karl, Mutti had dated a retired fire inspector named Eric Bluitt, and I'd been a little paranoid she was using his detective skills to find out once-and-for-all if her sweet son really was the arsonist responsible for the infamous Dofasco mail room fire of 2000. But I'm not an arsonist, not that I know of, and I'd told her that a thousand times. Eric had wanted to move in with Mutti, but she wasn't interested in a live-in partner after losing my dad, Leon. He was the love of her life. In 1950, at age eighteen, they'd married, and immigrated from Germany. They'd almost given up trying to have kids and were considering adoption when the universe finally answered their prayers and blessed them with a son, me, Norbert Reingruber. Eleven years later, Dad died from lung cancer. They had twenty-four years together, but it wasn't enough. Mutti never got over it. And, truthfully, neither did I.

Frustrated, Eric had hit the road. I wasn't surprised. I'd always felt he was a narcissist—but different than Donny, who was a good-hearted narcissist, if there is such a thing. Eric's favourite topic of conversation was always Eric, and that had gotten old real quick.

Behind Mutti, on the wall, there was a picture of Dad with his coworkers at the old Bick's Pickle Factory downtown on Parkdale Avenue. He was accepting a plaque for ten years of dedicated service. He'd been a plant foreman. I felt the familiar pang whenever I saw that picture. I really missed my dad. The Village wasn't the same without him.

The Village, which is really just a big chunk of East Hamilton Mountain, is the area around Flux Road and Steel Street. The four corners are filled with old strip malls. There's the Irondale Bowling Alley, the Blue Ball Tavern, the Irondale Library, Super Affordable Burial & Cremation Services, Jimmy's Barber Shop, and a bunch of other small businesses. The Village fans out for maybe four-square-kilometres, in John Pappas's estimate, although he's a bit of a know-it-all, so maybe he's not so right about that.

Tony thinks it's smaller than that, and Donny has a thousand different opinions on the subject, all of them constantly changing, of course, and we all argue constantly about the Village boundaries over coffee and donuts at Tim Hortons. And nobody else calls it the "Village". It's kind of our made-up name for just a regular old neighbourhood, in a medium-sized steel town. But I will say this—the Village has always been a great place to grow up and never leave. It feels right living here. I love the war-time bungalows, the way home owners keep them neatly groomed and upgraded, plus there's tons of great schools here, like Irondale Collegiate, and lots of green space, and old friends to hang out with. About a year ago, not long after Steven Dundee's comeback concert, Tony got it into his head to sarcastically name the corner of Flux Road and Steel Street "The Village" because, to him, it's a shitty collection of tired businesses that should have been demolished decades ago. But I disagree, and so do Donny and John, although John's right when he says some of the stores could use a facelift. Maybe you'd have to have grown up here to appreciate Tony's joke. And to love it like I do.

It was pretty darn obvious to me how Mutti felt about Karl. When she saw him, her eyes not only lit up, they twinkled! But, right from the get-go, Mutti had made it clear to Karl that they would only date on Friday nights, and if Karl wanted, he could stay over at her house, and he always did. She'd cook breakfast and dinner and then give him the boot. Before leaving, he always performed one of his trademark magic tricks, as a way to dramatically cap off their time together.

When he performed his magic act, he'd wear this cape, like a nerdy Dracula, black silk, red lining, with a red bowtie and shiny black top hat. It made me think of The Screw's fedora. *Fuzz me*! *I don't want to think about The Screw!* His trademark spell word was

"*Shhazammmy-zam-zam!*" He'd raise his eyebrows as if he was just as surprised as Mutti that his magic trick worked.

I grit my teeth. I found myself staring angrily at Karl—when Dad was alive, Mutti had a no-hat rule in the house, but now something about Karl had flipped a switch in her brain and she suddenly didn't care anymore. So, his cape and hat were cool, but my red tights were silly, were they? I tried not to let sudden anger in my belly take over. I told myself I wasn't mad at Karl. I was mad at The Screw. Actually, I was *terrified* of The Screw.

Karl forked crab cakes onto his plate and raised one up in front of Mutti. He circled his hand over it, and made it disappear. "*Shazammmy-zam-zam!*" Her eyes lit up. She was really impressed. *Karl's actually pretty good*, I thought, *despite the fact that he's a total weirdo and a nerd. But Mutti could do so much better.*

Then I reminded myself that *I* was a total weirdo and a nerd, and that Morag could do so much better. I felt a little ashamed for being a hypocrite.

"Maybe Karl the Great will perform a special bedroom magic trick for his sweetheart Anna next Friday." He arched an eyebrow at Mutti, and she blushed and made a strange face, one I definitely hadn't seen before and prayed would never see again.

"Gross," I muttered. I looked over at Morag, who was trying not to grin.

Mutti went all serious and fixed her gaze on Morag. "Eat, Morag, you're wasting away!"

Morag laughed. "That's very kind of you, Mutti, and entirely not true." She smiled at her mother-in-law as she spooned corn onto her plate.

I loved Morag's figure. She was totally voluptuous.

I'd piled my plate to overflowing, a bad habit for sure, and I was eating so fast Morag had stopped with her fork half-way to her mouth and stared at me.

"Slow down, babe. Take a breath."

I'd slipped into a deep, churning mind-hole, imagining The Screw doing nasty things to me and my loved ones.

I looked at Morag for reassurance. "Sorry."

She smiled at me and went back to eating.

Despite my unhealthy eating, lack of exercise, and Fred Flintstone gut, Morag really loved me, and that's exactly the reason why I didn't miss the single life, living in Mutti's basement apartment, with my rock posters and bar fridge and big screen tv. All that seemed small and unimportant to me now. Once in awhile, I got nostalgic, but I never wanted to go back to those days. My life with Morag was a million times better.

I forked a crab cake into my mouth. After one bite, I flinched.

"Mutti? Are these *crab* cakes? They taste...unusual."

Everyone had slowed their chewing, and I could tell they had known but didn't want to offend the chef. Leave it to me to open my big mouth.

A light bulb went off in Mutti's head, and she let out a little gasp. "Oh, I'm so sorry. I guess I was distracted. It's a new recipe and I think I scooped in sauerkraut instead of crab."

Karl playfully wagged his finger at her. "Anna, you're full of surprises, you little hottie." He edged his super pale face close to hers like a vampire hopped up on Viagra and Romance. "Karl the Great forgives your sweet transgression." He kissed her hand, gently. "Your crab cakes are scrumptious, my dear, I adore them."

"Get a room, you two," I said. "You're grossing me the heck out. *Blecch.*"

"Karl's right," Morag said, cheerfully. "They really are scrumptious." She was nodding at Mutti, and tilted her head at me to do the same. Then she kicked me beneath the table, and I nodded too, forcing a smile onto my face. "Taste great, Mutti, they really do."

"Oh, you're all too kind," she said, her face crinkling as she took a bite. "But don't feel you have to eat it!" She chewed and swallowed. "Oh dear, they do taste awful!" Norbie, maybe you and your friends can used them as hockey pucks."

Everyone laughed at Anna's joke.

But I thought I'd detected an unfamiliar note of sadness in Mutti's eyes. For the first time, I noticed the age spots on her cheeks, and the dark bags under her eyes. How had I missed really seeing those?

Suddenly, the dining room felt like a tomb stuffed with old family portraits, tacky orange Sixties' wallpaper, and a dusty spoon rack full of tarnished silver spoons that made me think of dead soldiers. The cobwebbed chandelier seemed dated, everything just old and tired. In that moment, I realized I couldn't *feel* my old home any longer, that I'd truly broken up with it the day I'd married Morag and moved out. Knowing I couldn't see everything the way I used to made me super sad. I felt another pang—I suddenly missed my dad in a way I hadn't in years.

"Hey, how did you make out at ComWorld?" Karl asked. His face was eager. "Sell much? Rub shoulders with the celebs?"

I didn't even feel like talking about the cosplayers, the panels, or even William Shatner. Not tonight. "Oh, uh, you know, sold a few books, gave away some merchandise. The usual newbie writer stuff, right, Morag?"

"Yep," she said, and downed half a glass of wine in a single gulp.

The wine went down the wrong way, and she started coughing. The stress of the day was clearly getting to her. I rubbed her back.

"Norbie, maybe next year I could rent a booth beside you and sell my magic kits. Think we could do that, eh? Karl the Great and Norbert Reingruber, together again, at last!" A big shiny grin lit up his face.

Together never! My insides sagged. I didn't want to hurt Karl's feelings, but I'd rather do time for imaginary arson than have

Karl-the-Vampire mugging beside me at a comic convention. Everyone knows you can't have magicians at ComWorld. I mean, get real!

"You never know, Karl," I said, finally. "You should inquire about that. I would do it for you, but I'm pretty busy these days." *Get outta here before you say something stupid to Karl and hurt Mutti's feelings.*

"Maybe next time Anna and I could go with you and Morag, make a day of it. Wouldn't that be a hoot?"

"Absolutely," I said. *Not*, I thought. Except apparently it came out of my big mouth.

"You muttered," Mutti said, tapping her fork against her plate, staring me down. "Now I know for sure something is wrong." She whispered to Karl. "My poor Norbert was born with a giant head, but that only made me love him more. And of course, with that big, giant brain came a *lot* of thoughts. It's a struggle for my boy."

Karl nodded sympathetically, sizing up my noggin.

I loved most things about Mutti, but it always bothered me when she brought up my head size. I knew she couldn't help it. But really, so *what* if my baby head was just a little big? It was perfectly fine now. Nothing to worry about.

So, I pretended I hadn't heard Mutti.

Beside the coffee table in the living room there was a large black box, one of Karl's stage props. "Another after-dinner magic trick, Karl?"

"Of course," he said. He never stopped smiling, as if he was a contestant in a smiling contest.

"Karl the Great," I said. "Constantly great."

"Norbert!" said Mutti, shocked at my sarcastic tone.

I sighed. "Sorry, Karl. I'm just off tonight."

Mutti smiled away my sarcasm, and gazed at Karl with love in her eyes. He smiled back at her. She found Karl's showmanship endearing, and, in the end, I was happy Karl made her happy.

She won't live forever, a familiar voice said inside me. I told it to buzz off.

By the time we were half way through dessert, Karl had become as animated as Donny would about a get-rich-quick scheme. Karl was rambling on about his glory days working his act on the cruise lines. I was only half-listening, when a black car pulled up to the front curb. The car's four-way flashers sprayed bloody red light all over the front lawn.

Be cool, I told myself, *people pull over all the time.* Probably someone trying to take a call on their cell phone. The Screw had given me till Tuesday to yank my books, so it was too early for him to try to kill me and my family. *Call Tye now and tell him to pull the books! Stop procrastinating!*

I stewed in anger. *No one screws with Mutti! Not even the Fuzzin' Screw!*

"Norbie," Mutti said gently, "there is something I need to tell you."

"Pardon?" I said, trying to dial out of my mind-hole. Finally, I met her gaze. I knew something was definitely off. I spoke before thinking. "Are you sure marrying Karl's a good decision?"

Morag gasped. She was giving me a look I knew very well. We'd be having a chat later, I could tell.

But Mutti wasn't offended. She chuckled quietly. "Dearest Norbert, we're not getting married. Well, not that I know of." She glanced briefly at Karl.

Karl's eyebrows shot up as if he couldn't believe his own ears. "We're not?" he said, half-jokingly.

Anna smiled at him. "That's *not* what I want to talk to Norbert about."

Outside, inside the black car, someone lit a cigarette. *Screw you, Screw!* My leg began pumping involuntarily. I dragged my attention back to my mother.

"Oh," Karl said. He looked like he knew what was coming next. He reached out and put a hand on her back.

Mutti nodded and faced me. Her eyes filled with compassion. "Back in March, I saw a specialist about some lower abdominal pain." She lowered her voice. "An MRI showed I have a tumour on my uterus. The good news is the specialist said she thinks she can remove it and I'll be back to my old self in no time flat." How could she speak those words calmly?

My world was collapsing around me. "Cancer, Mutti?" Wow. Uterine cancer. *Oh jeee. Oh holy crap.*

"Norbert, dear," she said, reaching across the table and taking my hand.

"I'll be okay. You don't need to worry about me. Focus on yourself, Mutti."

"When's your surgery date?" Morag asked. Her eyes were red.

"Tuesday. Eleven a.m."

"Tuesday?" I squeaked. "Oh man! Why didn't you tell me sooner, Mutti?"

"Norbert, I didn't want you worrying for months on end."

In the space of a few minutes, I'd gone from forty to four, just a vulnerable little boy, afraid his mom was going to die. This was one of my worst fears, coming true.

Then the nasty thought suddenly occurred to me. I suddenly realized The Screw's deadline was *two hours* before Mutti's surgery. What were the odds? Panic played a psychotic bongo rhythm in my gut. I thought: *What if The Screw kills us before Mutti's surgery? What about her tumour? She'll be dead you idiot! What will it matter then?*

"Time for my magic trick!" Karl announced, trying to lighten the mood. He slid his chair back from the table. "You're going to love this one, Anna, you too, Morag. Norbie," he said, pointing at me, "this trick will blow your mind."

Mutti gave me a reassuring smile. "Don't worry Norbert, I'll be fine. A routine operation, you'll see."

"I'll drive you to the hospital, and I won't take no for an answer."

"Thanks, Norbert. You are a very good son."

I pawed at the tears pooling in my eyes. Mutti's words—the surgeon's words—echoed inside my head: *Thinks she can remove it.* That didn't sound so great. *Thinks* was a lot different than *knows*.

Morag rubbed my back and searched my face. "Hang in there, big guy. We have to trust everything will work out just fine for Mutti."

I nodded, although I wasn't ready to trust.

Karl practically skipped into the living room, cape flowing behind him. He flicked off the main lights, dragged a floor lamp close to the coffee table, positioned it like a spotlight, and flicked it on. It lit up the black box. He slid off the lid and waved his magic wand over it.

"Ladies and Gentleman, welcome to the greatest magic show on Earth! I am Karl the Great, and tonight I present to you, for the first time *ever*, at the lovely Anna Reingruber's Steeltown Palace, a very special magic trick!" His eyes expanded to the size of saucers.

Mutti and Morag clapped. I couldn't even *fake* fake enthusiasm. My whole body shook. I stared down at my pudgy hands drumming the table—*are those my hands?*—and I swear flames were shooting up behind my eyes like MegaFreak pyrotechnics, and I didn't even see Karl, I was staring so hard past him, through the window, at the mystery car.

Morag touched my shoulder. "Norbie, what's wrong, babe?"

I shoved away from the table, my chair noisily scraping the floor. A serving dish rattled onto the floor, tossing crab cakes.

Karl froze, but when he realized he wasn't my target he slipped seamlessly back into his act, since the show must go on.

"Where are you going, Norbert?" Mutti asked, jumping out of her chair after me.

"*Shazammmy-zam-zam!*" Karl cried, but then all at once his excitement withered. "What? What's going on?"

Poor Karl. I tore past him. He arched away from me, freaked out. Morag told me later that I'd run past him so fast I'd flapped his cape.

I had never felt so scared, furious, or determined, not even the time I'd studied ten days in a row for a Grade Twelve math exam, only to find out a week later I'd barely passed. And boy, did *that* make me angry. Even John Pappas hadn't ever made me this angry, and that was really saying something.

I bolted out the front door.

It was a big black muscle car. A car Tony would be hot to drive. But as I ran up to it, it drove off, slowly speeding up, its throttling engine so loud I swear it was cracking the bricks of the bungalows lining the street.

"Come back and fight like a man!" I yelled, sprinting after it in my stocking-feet. My Superman socks gave me an extra jolt of energy and resolve.

In sprint, I was always super-fast for the first one-hundred metres, had been since elementary school, but after that I totally gassed out. I ran like Humpty Dumpty, if Humpty had a sugar rush, and as mean as that sounds, I'm okay saying that about myself. It was better than John name-calling me, which he did *often*.

I was huffing and puffing, and my stocking feet were pounding the pavement. I so wanted to smash my fist through The Screw's precious car.

As expected, at the hundred-metre mark, I was running on fumes.

How will you protect Morag if you can't run the distance? said that shitty familiar voice inside my head.

I will! I answered. *You'll see! I'll go on a diet when this is all over and hit the gym and I'll do wind sprints every second day and then I'll train for a marathon.*

I was bent double, gasping for breath, staring up at the car roaring away. I could barely make out two shadowy figures, one hulking in the passenger seat, another in the back. Whoever was driving was short. Poking above the driver's seat was the top half of a fedora.

The driver rolled the window down. A hand reached out and flipped me the bird.

And I realized I was trembling, like a school kid who's just realized his mistake, a split second after standing up to a bully twice his size.

Chapter 3

I was on the phone with Mutti. I threw open the window facing Flux Road, hoping to draw fresh air into our stuffy apartment. Outside our window, the Irondale Bowling Alley sign pulsed neon twenty-four/seven. Twelve hours a day, Morag and I could hear the muffled sounds of bowling balls, but after a few months, it had become like one of those white noise machines for us, just comforting background noise.

Workers had shown up to tar the strip mall roof. When I was younger, Sundays had been a day of rest. Man, the world had definitely changed. Normally, I loved the reek of hot tar, but today it stunk up the apartment so bad I had to shut the window.

The roofer's boots were clomping on the roof, and The Pussy Cat Dolls were singing, "When I Grow Up" on the radio. I had to turn it down to better hear Mutti on the phone.

Morag was just about vibrating in her new Spock t-shirt. Behind her, on the kitchen counter, was yesterday's pile of dirty breakfast dishes. "No, no, no," she hissed at me. She jabbed a finger on my chest. "No guns, Norbie, you know I hate guns! A simple phone call will fix this! Norbie, we talked about this yesterday on the bus, we agreed on this. Remember?"

I pressed my mitt against the phone so Mutti wouldn't hear. "I don't like guns either, Morag, but I need Dad's Luger to protect everybody."

"No guns!" She crossed her arms tight against her chest.

"Okay, okay, have it your way." I took a slow, deep breath, and continued my awkward conversation with my mother. "Oh, no, I was just wondering, Mutti." I laughed hollowly. "Thought maybe we can sell it on Ebay or something. Or give it to the Hamilton Historical Society. Kinda dangerous having a Luger in the house. I mean, what if it goes go off on its own? I mean, it's so old and everything, right? Or what if a thief breaks in and uses it against you?" I mopped away the perspiration on my face. "No, Mutti, I'm not over-reacting. There've been a lot of break-ins in Hamilton recently. Crackheads desperate for quick money, that kind of thing." My words flew out of my mouth. "Anyway, thanks so much again for dinner, Mutti, it was superb. Sorry I ran out. As I said, that racoon was digging up your planters. Next time we'll stick around for a longer visit and we'll do the dishes. And tell Karl we look forward to seeing his next magic trick. I'm sure it'll be a doozy. And please call if you need anything, okay? *Anything*...Yes, I love you, too."

After I hung up, I couldn't stop the crazy storm of worry in my head.

"Calm down," Morag ordered me. "And call Tye. *Now!*"

She plopped down beside me on the old green couch Mutti had given us, the same one I'd crashed on with my old buds in my basement apartment. It was hard to say no to Morag, especially when she was wearing a t-shirt and not much else. At least that was one good thing about the summer heat in our little apartment.

I found myself distractedly toying with my boyhood harmonica. I hadn't played it in years, and I was rusty as heck. For some reason, I began playing, "When The Saints Go Marching In."

Morag winced—my playing was that bad. She rested her hand on my thigh. I let the harmonica drift down to my lap.

"Babe, you and I both know you procrastinate when you're scared or afraid to disappoint. But you have to man up on this one, Norbie. It's crucial. So call Tye and order him to yank the books." She squeezed my hand. "You can do this."

"All our hard work, Morag," I said quietly, "down the tubes!" I raised my voice. "All because of that piece of garbage!"

Desperate for comfort, I snatched up my old Steven scrapbook from the coffee table and stared at the photo of him backing out of his parents' driveway. It always gave me a pang. *Stop saving the world for just a while, Steven, and come home and save me, your old buddy, and almost best friend, Norbert Reingruber. I know you're not a real superhero, man, but jeez, I sure could use one right now. If I was any fuzzin' good, I would be a fuzzin' hero, instead of wishing somebody else would rescue me.*

"We'll make an even better comic book, Norbie," Morag said. "If this Shadow guy doesn't like Doctor Derangio, you'll come up with a better villain. And you'll dream up a weapon just as good, if not better than the Invisiblator. Whatever it is about the Steeltown Avenger that this guy doesn't like, we'll get rid of. The next one will be awesome. If Tye Novak signed you, it means he believes in you. He wouldn't have signed you unless he recognized your talent." She leaned her cheek against mine and squeezed my hand.

"*Our* talent," I said. "You wrote this comic, too, Morag. But I'm worried. I mean, we signed a contract. What if Tye doesn't let us out? What if he takes us to court and sues the pants off us? Not that we have anything worth taking."

"Tell him the truth, Norbie. He'll understand." Would he? I hoped Morag was right, but my brain was a giant Jiffy Pop of fear.

I dialed and waited. I held the phone away from my ear. "You know what? It's early. I should call him during business hours." I went to hang up, but Morag stopped me.

"He'll understand." She pushed my phone hand back to my ear.

"Hello?" Tye's voice.

"Oh, hi, Tye, um, it's me, Norbert Reingruber, your new comic book writer." I bit my lip. *He already knows that, you blockhead!*

I explained to Tye how an evil dwarf named The Screw had threatened to kill me and my family if I didn't pull the comic books by Tuesday morning at eleven; how there was a real Invisiblator used by a real master criminal called Shadow, and that I'd accidentally cooked up a similar device in my comic book. "Can you believe it, Tye? What are the odds?" I laughed nervously, searching Morag's face for a lifeline. She wasn't cutting me any slack.

Tye reacted pretty badly.

"Imposter syndrome? No, of course I don't—...'A kick-ass conductor on my personal success train?' Uh—...Okay, uh, I'll read that. Let me write that down. Tony Robbins. *Awaken the Giant Within.* Is that a fantasy novel?...The Screw *is* real, Tye, Scout's Honour...Hey! I don't do LSD, and no I don't want to try 'shrooms...Shadow *could* be real...My family's lives are in danger, Tye, so we *have* to pull the books!...How many? Thirty-six cities!...Of course I *do* want to honour the contract, but—... Please don't hang up...Tye, this isn't a joke! I—!"

My skin was clammy. My vision misty.

"What are we going to do, Norbie?" Morag said, firmly, making me blink.

I licked my lips as if discovering them for the first time. She straddled me, and cradled my huge head in her small hands. She stared deep into my eyes. "How bad *is* it?"

"Bad, real bad. Well, you probably got most of it, right? Yesterday, Tye shipped five thousand books to stores on the West coast. And the book's in bookstores in thirty-six cities. Can you believe that? Heh heh. *The Steeltown Avenger* is blowing up! Great timing. Our dream is coming true, just in time for our gruesome murder. Tye said in his twenty years as a publisher, he's never seen a comic book so fast out of the gates. It's like he doesn't want to believe what I'm telling him, or he can't believe it. Of course, it *does* sound completely insane."

"Now don't get mad, Norbie," Morag said, gently stroking my beard, "but are you one hundred percent sure you're not imagining The Screw? Like the time you said Batman was real and when I tried to change your mind, you got mad at me?"

"I *didn't* imagine him Morag!" I squeaked. "And I never said Batman was real, only he *could* be real." *At least that's what I think I said.*

The look on Morag's face suddenly changed. "I'm scared, Norbie," she said, and she lunge-hugged me.

"I'll Kung Fu his butt if he tries anything with you or Mutti!"

"I know you will." She inhaled deeply. "But I'm really scared for you, too."

I could tell by the tone of her voice she was referring to my mental health. I didn't like how that made me feel.

She spoke softly into my ear. "I think the pressure of running the store and dealing with this comic book success has taken its toll on you. I'm afraid you'll end up like Donny. He's always imagining stuff that isn't real and, like a crazy man, he actually acts on it. Most of the time, Allison's beside herself, with her lawyer on speed dial and one foot out the door of their marriage. I don't know which is worse—that you've imagined The Screw, or that he's real."

"Morag, for the last time, I'm *not* making him up, and I'm not going to end up like Donny. He's a total fuzzin' fruitcake! And I'm not!" My blood was boiling. I wasn't mad at Morag, I was mad at my situation, and, of course, Donny. Because, one way or another, Donny Love had been a fuzzin' pain in my butt for four decades.

A knock at the door freaked me out. I bolted up so fast I knocked Morag to the floor. I was in Tiger Pose so fast, Bruce Lee would have been proud. I waited to hear The Screw's voice before I flying front-kicked through our door and destroyed him.

"Norbert Reingruber," came the voice, "open up immediately! This is your Dungeon Master speaking!"

Donny? Not now, you fuzzin' weirdo!

Morag shook her head briskly at me to stay quiet. Tonight was our weekly games night—I'd totally forgotten about it I was so stressed out—but playing Dungeons and Dragons with Donny was the last thing I needed. No way was I up to his half-baked ideas about this and that tonight. Since moving back to Hamilton, he'd really gone downhill.

"I know you're in there, Norbster. I can hear you breathing. Thought we'd shake things up a little tonight. Brought Risk Transformers Cybertron Battle Edition, and a party size bag of cheese puffs. You know how much you love cheese puffs, Norbster. Yum-yum-yum!"

I began licking my lips. I was salivating. *He's trying to break me, he knows how much I love cheese puffs. Fuck you, Donny Love! I mean, fuzz you!*

Morag saw that, as usual, I was on the verge of cracking under Donny's high-pressure sales tactics, so she pressed a hand over my mouth. Although I was trembling with fear, and anger, and hunger, I didn't crack. Donny continued with his Chinese water torture. *Drip.* "Mmm. These puffs taste *sooo* fresh." He'd opened the bag and was wafting it near the door jam. *Drip.* Crunch Crunch Crunch. "Oh my God, these are those new cheesier ones. Awesome recipe upgrade." *Drip.* "You can be the purple game pieces, Norb."

Fuzz you, Love! He knew I loved the purple pieces.

"OK, no hard feelings," Donny said, finally. "Let's try again next week." He clomped away from the door and down the hallway. "Who loves ya, baby!"

I dealt with my stress in typical fashion. I escaped into an imaginary world of my own devising, this time envisioning myself as Spiderman perched on the edge of the bowling alley rooftop, shooting my web into the parking lot below, ensnaring The Screw and his evil henchmen. I even conjured up a wail of sirens, as Hamilton's finest pulled in and arrested the evil-doers and thanked me for being an excellent citizen. *Spiderman strikes again!*

Morag saw that I'd plunged down into my predictable rabbit hole and so pinched me awake.

She used a tissue to mop away the sweat on my forehead. I hadn't realized I'd been sweating. Slowly, the fog of my imaginary world lifted and I found myself stuck in the reality of my nightmare.

Chapter 4

"YOU WANT US TO BE THERE for you when *shit goes down*?" Tony said, "And what kind of shit are we talking about, exactly? Elves? Hobbits?" He shook his head. "Norb, man, you're frickin' crazier than Donny."

Tony laughed, but then he choked on a piece of sour cream glazed donut. He did this a lot. He was an intense guy. As usual, his face turned beet red. Donut crumbs flew out of his mouth onto his white Village Idiots hockey jersey. He waved us off from even thinking about giving him the Heimlich maneuver, which we always offered whenever he was choking on his food. Tony would be offended if anyone saved his life. A real man should save his own, apparently. Eventually, as always, he cleared his own throat.

We were sitting at our usual table at Tim's Horton's, after our weekly Sunday morning road hockey game in the Irondale Collegiate parking lot. Today, we'd beat another Village team, the Iron Street Bullies, four to three. I'd foiled a potential game-tying goal by stopping a slap shot with a flick of my big head. That had gotten a really big cheer from the guys. It had gotten me a slight headache, too. I was voted MVP. When playing hockey, my big head was a huge asset. That was basically the only time.

Morag had made me go that morning. She'd said I needed to get some exercise, blow off some steam. She was probably right. Plus, I figured she needed a break from me and my contagious craziness for a couple of hours.

It had been John's idea to call ourselves the Village Idiots. Three years ago we'd joined the Hamilton Hammers Ball Hockey League, ages thirty-five and up, and it was the best decision we'd made as a group in a really long time. There were seven guys on our team: me, Donny, Tony, and John, plus three other guys from high school. There were a total of twelve teams in the league.

I had no clue what was happening in the world of pro hockey, but I knew almost every stat linked to *our* league. I liked it when my friends patted me on the back after I'd made a big save. People always seemed so shocked by how nimble I was for such a big, oafy guy. I'd also designed our logo and jerseys. I wore number 1, after the greatest goalie of all time, Maple Leafs Johnny Bower. I'd been a huge NHL fan until sixteen when I'd suddenly flipped for comics and art and writing. But I still loved to play. John wore number 27, in honour of Montreal legend Frank Mahovlich, and Donny wore number 29 in honour of Ken Dryden. Tony, like me, was an ardent Leafs fan— he wore Davey Keon's number 14. I guess there was still some kid in all of us.

Our after-game Sunday morning ritual was hanging out at the coffee shop. I loved this part of the week. I loved spending time with *The Fellowship*, as I'd come to think of us.

I knew that telling my buds about The Screw was dumb. I knew they'd think I was nuts. But that was the thing of it—I was co-dependent on them, had always been that way. I'd always been afraid to make big decisions without their good opinion. I couldn't help myself. I had developed some insight, thanks to Morag, but clearly not enough to totally change. Maybe one day I would make my own decisions. I really hoped so. For that day, I was a pathetic forty-year-old, stuck in a donut shop, waiting for his old high school buds to tell him exactly how he should save his family.

Donny was on his way. First, he had to pick up diapers and drop them off at home for Allison.

I thought back to last night. After Donny'd left, Morag and I had worked ourselves up into a real lather, neither of us able to console each other or form a plan we could both agree on. After awhile, Morag did what she always did when totally stressed out—she binge-watched *The X-Files* and ate Doritos. I'd hopped on my Vespa scooter, and patrolled a circuit of the sidewalk in front of Mutti's house and the bowling alley parking lot, to make sure The Screw and his thugs weren't coming to kill us before the deadline.

I must have stopped at least five times to buy snacks—Humpty Dumpty barbecue chips and chili dogs at the 7-11 convenience store beside the Shell gas station. Morag would have vetoed the chili dogs. She always suspected those dogs rolled around on that grill for days on end. But patrolling and fear had really cranked up my appetite. Luckily for The Screw, he'd stayed out of my face or I would have busted him a new one. Chips and dogs can really give a guy a lot of extra energy.

"Norb," John said, "snap out of it, bud. You've gone to a strange land in a far-away place."

Oops. "Oh, sorry about that."

John had crossed his legs at the knee, and was bobbing a gleaming dress shoe in the air. It was long and pointy and very stylish. He was always shiny and well-groomed and on-the-move. John never had a stray nose hair. I always felt like a water buffalo next to him.

Even when John played road hockey, he wore his shiny shoes. He claimed they helped him skate along the road. We couldn't argue with that. He *actually* glided, and, not only that, he scored goals!

"So, let me get this straight. An evil guy called The Screw works for an evil boss called Shadow, and you created a fictional Invisiblator weapon, which just happens to be a real device invented by Shadow for evil purposes?" He raised his eyebrows another notch. "And now you've got seventy-two hours to remove all traces of your comic or he'll cap your family?" He looked at Tony, who was doing his best to hide his annoyance and not hurt my feelings. But I could tell he thought I was crazy.

John sighed. "Norb, this is exactly why your name is Eggie. You say the same crazy things you did in high school." He sipped his coffee. "I'm honestly worried about you." He smirked at me.

"Man, you know I hate it when you call me Eggie," I said.

"Too bad for you, Eggie."

"Shut up, Pappas," I muttered.

"Sorry," John said, totally insincere. "It slipped out. I apologize."

"C'mon guys, what are you, twelve?" Tony managed to sound like our dad.

And there we were again, for a brief moment acting like adolescents, Tony acting as referee. I took a long angry haul on my four-by-four coffee—four creams four sugars—and scalded my mouth.

I loved John and Tony, but since marrying Morag, I was losing patience with them, especially John. Why did he think he had the right to name-call me, like were still the same goofy, pimple-faced teenagers trading jibes in the high school cafeteria?

I had thought that getting published and marrying Morag would have earned me my friends' respect. But it didn't. *Maybe they're jealous*, I thought. And then I had to take a deep breath, because, as crazy as that sounded, it could be true. Maybe they didn't like the changes in me, in my life. Maybe they preferred dorky, loser Norb, because—because *why*? I didn't want to think about that right now.

"So who is this Shadow meatball?" Tony asked through a mouthful of donut. He was chewing more carefully now. "Is he reality real, or comic book real?"

"Reality real," I said, pawing crumbs from my beard. "An evil scientist bent on world domination. At least, that's what I've been able to surmise. And I'm pretty sure it's my Invisiblator he's mad about."

John chortled. "An evil scientist bent on world domination? So he uses a real *Invisiblator* to make himself invisible so he can do whatever he wants and take over the world?" He rolled his eyes.

"Listen Papsmear, I—" I exhaled hard. I immediately regretted using my old juvenile nickname for John. Now who was the bumhead?

"Listen, John, if you read my comic book you'd realized that's not how an Invisiblator works. And he probably doesn't call his machine an "Invisiblator". I mean, that's just my term for it. I keep trying to tell you,

you can learn a lot from comic books, if you just took the time to read them."

He raised an eyebrow. "Tell me more about this thing."

"It's a hand held-device. It shoots out a ray and renders a human invisible for three hours."

"I can think of a few people I'd like to try that on," Tony said, grimacing.

John was grinning. The bright overhead light was glinting in his perfect white teeth. "Just think of the possibilities. An invisible man could have a lot of fun with the *ladies*."

Tony shot him a look of reproach.

John shrugged it off.

"Listen!" I pounded the table, sloshing coffee out of my cup, spilling crumbs off the table onto the floor. The old couple beside us stared, but I didn't care. "You guys have to help me! By nine o'clock Tuesday morning, all my books have to be out of stores. If they aren't, The Screw kills my family!" I stared hard at Tony. "In other words, *shit goes down*."

"Easy, cowboy," Elise, the shift manager, called over from behind the counter. We were on a first-name basis with Elise. She was older than the hills and tough as a North End scrapper. She'd been slinging coffee and donuts for forty years in this very location. She'd even known my dad. But she was always pretty nice to us.

"Sorry, Elise," we automatically called back.

I could see Tony was trying to figure out whether he believed me. "And how do you propose we do that, Norb?" he said. "Where *are* your comic books?"

"In U.S. comic book shops." I sagged.

Tony threw up his hands. "*Pfft*. Good luck with that!"

"Norb," John said, leaning across the table, "we can't just hop on a plane and fly across the border and extract—which, by the way, means what? Buy? Steal?—your books from countless comic book shops before Tuesday morning. And even if we could miraculously pull it off, which we can't, are you going to pay for our plane fares and meals and time missed at work?" He shrugged. "Why don't you get your publisher on the phone and tell him to order his salespeople to physically yank the comics. Or better yet, get them to call the shops. Easy-peasy."

I fell silent. I didn't want to tell them because I knew how they'd react. But what choice did I have? I swallowed, then I told them about my call with Tye Novak.

"Imposter Syndrome?" Tony said, shifting in his chair. "Hope that's not the same thing as frickin' *Crazy Syndrome*, which Donny has in spades. Speaking of Donny, we should discuss his latest act of desperation before he gets here, but not now. I don't have the stomach for it."

"What has he done now?"

Tony just shook his head.

"Norb," John said. "I don't think working in your shop is good for you. The impact of working in a store full of fantasy and then writing fantasies after work would do a number on anyone's mental well-being. Maybe hire a lawyer and see if he can't get you your old job at Dofasco. Working there will ground you back in reality, and then you can write your books at night with a clear mind. You don't want to end up like Donny, creating delusions in your head and acting on them."

For a change, John wasn't smirking. He looked genuinely concerned for me, even if his concern was misplaced. John didn't know a lot about writing. It wasn't his fault, so I didn't get mad at him.

"Thanks, John, I'll consider that."

Tony, as usual, had been knifing his hand across his throat, silently telling John to shut his pie hole about Dofasco. I sighed and shook my head. Tony and John had played out this scenario at least a hundred times since I'd been fired from Dofasco. The steelmakers had accused me of setting their mailroom on fire, but they couldn't find enough evidence, so the police hadn't laid any charges. I was *almost* sure I was innocent. Luckily, not long afterwards, I'd scored a job working part-time at Talbot's Trading Card Shop beside the bowling alley, a place I felt I actually belonged. The pay was terrible but the job was awesome. It had just been the fresh start I'd needed.

"Have you considered seeing a shrink?" John said, with way less sarcasm than usual. "Just to make sure The Screw isn't a paranoid delusion? I'm being serious, okay?"

My ears burned. I began trembling. "The Screw isn't a paranoid delusion."

John nodded solemnly at me. "Morag should have a medical plan working for the City. My sister works in the Records Department, and she has one. They offer five hundred bucks a year for counselling. You should grab a piece of that, Norb."

John glanced over at Tony, who was busy thumbing an issue of *Hot Rod* magazine. He'd checked out of the conversation.

I felt the blood rush into my cheeks. "You guys never take me seriously! I could sell a million comic books and you guys still wouldn't respect me. And," I said, twisting my beard, "you don't believe me when I tell you the truth, despite the fact I *always* tell you the truth. I lowered my voice. "Come on, guys, you're supposed to be my friends!"

Tony looked up from his magazine, softening. "The truth, Norb? Like that time Steven was buried in that cemetery down in Jordan, but he clearly wasn't? Was that the truth?" He added: "And yes, we *are* your friends Norb, obviously."

"That was your cousin's mistake, not mine! Anyway, all three of you keep trying to lock me inside a time capsule. It's like you don't want me to change, or succeed. I'm not the Norbie I once was, okay? I'm married—to a total babe, by the way—I'm a writer, a business-owner, and I'm going to start a family, and I'm definitely not making crap up about The Screw! So deal with it, Nascar Tony!" I was gasping a little now. "And, for the last time, I'm pretty sure I didn't set the mailroom on fire!"

"Shut your hole," an old guy crowed from his scooter two tables over. "I can't hear myself fucking think."

"Sorry," I mouthed.

John burst out laughing, his lovely teeth lighting up the donut shop. He saw that he had an audience so he leaned back in his chair and pointed at me, as if to say he had nothing to do with Santa's meltdown.

"'I'm not the Norbie I once was?'" Tony said. "For real, Norb? You sound like Scrooge from *A Christmas Carol!*" He palmed his forehead. "Jesus, only a loser would still be hanging out with his loser friends from high school." He sighed. "And speaking of losers, where the frig' is Donny? It's his turn to buy."

Elise shot us the stink eye. John shot Tony the stink eye. I shot them both the stink eye. It was not a happy coffee shop.

Tony eyed me skeptically. "Okay Norb, here's how I'll help you. If *you* can't get your books off the shelves by Tuesday, you and Morag and your mom can stay in my basement for a few days. By the way, congrats on the comic book deal, Norb. I know how much it means to you, even though I don't understand any of it."

Tony looked pretty embarrassed. He finished off his third donut in record time and went back to reading his magazine.

My leg was pumping involuntarily.

"I'll help, too, Norb," John said, grinning. "I'll have a dance-off with The Screw outside the bowling alley. If I win, which I'm pretty sure I will, he agrees to leave you alone." He laughed, cockily bobbing his shiny shoe in the air.

"Grow up, Pap*ass*!" I said, clenching my fists.

"Oh no you don't!" Elise yelled from the counter. "No damn way, buddy, not on my shift!"

She stormed out from behind the counter. We all actually flinched, thinking she was coming for us, but she flew past us, out the main doors.

Tony smacked his magazine against the table. "Aww, Christ, what now?"

Outside the main window, beside his son's stroller, Donny Love was busking, strumming his acoustic guitar. We could hear his voice through the window glass. As usual, he was singing off-key. His face was beet red as he belted out one of his mediocre original songs—"Everyone Loves the Hammer"—which he'd been hawking on Bandcamp with zero success.

Once again, it's the Donny Love Show. And everyone will forget about helping me because he's stealing the fuzzin' spotlight.

He was still wearing his dumb *Making Steven Famous* ball cap. Two weeks ago, he'd bought an insanely expensive billboard ad in the heart of the Village, promoting his new book. Doing that had gotten him into a heap of trouble with Allison, and potentially, Steven. Last fall, he'd gone totally off the rails, written some seriously crazy lies about our old friend Steven in our local newspaper, and almost blown up his life. He barely saved his marriage. Then he settled down for a while. Until the hat and the songs and the billboard. What the hell was wrong with him?

Until two weeks ago, we had had no idea he'd been writing a book about all that insanity, which was weird, because he usually talked incessantly about himself and his projects. Newspaper columnist. Liar. Novelist. Now singer-songwriter? *What next? Dog walker? Porn star? Professional whistler?* He hadn't even used his own name on this novel. He'd stolen the name of a guy we'd gone to school with. At least I'd had the guts to write *The Steeltown Avenger* under my own name.

My stomach dropped when I saw a Ticats cap plunked down for donations on the concrete in front of him. Had he been fired? *What's wrong with you, Love? You're lucky I don't call Children's Aid, you fuzzin' idiot!*

Chapter 5

I WATCHED ELISE HOVER her palm over her opposite shoulder and knife the other forward, signalling a foul. Donny slumped and nodded. This wasn't the first time Elise had set him straight at Hortons. He knew the routine.

Frowning, she swung open the door and jerked her head. He quickly gathered up his hat and pushed the stroller inside, his guitar twanging against the glass.

The folks inside applauded, not for his crappy performance, but for Elise for making him shut up so they could eat and drink in peace. Citizens of Hamilton can take a lot of abuse, but there are limits, you know?

I smiled at Stewart as Donny plopped down at our table. Stewart really was a cute, adorable kid. In the past few months, I'd found myself thinking about having babies with Morag, curly-haired, red-headed babies, who'd call me "Dada" and stuff. This was a totally new daydream for me. And a little tiny part of me thought I might actually make a halfway-okay dad. At least, with Morag as their mom, our kids would be halfway to awesome.

Donny came to the table with a coffee and a French cruller, plus a Timbit for the baby. His pupils were the size of pie plates. "Allison's not feeling well so she asked me to look after Stewart. I knew I shouldn't busk with him, guys, but I couldn't help myself. Don't judge, okay? I've got to promote my new album. It's urgent, man." He was talking at hyper-speed, the way he always did when he was hopped up, which was most of the time. It was a really good thing he didn't do drugs. Not long after last year's scandal, Donny's mental health had worsened. He'd become manic, and we'd figured all that had something to do with the stress of moving back to Hamilton and raising a toddler, coupled with financial stress. He had to pay off a huge debt after all the money he'd spent on the big reunion concert/giant scam last year. We wondered if he'd stopped taking his medication, although we had no real idea if he even had meds or had a diagnosis. That was typical of our group of friends. We talked around each other's problems. We didn't have the courage to talk to each other properly, heart-to-heart.

Whenever John asked him if he was taking medication or suggested maybe he should for his family's sake, Donny got really angry and sullen, so John would eventually back off.

"Stewart's growing so fast," I said. Then I glowered at Donny and lowered my voice. "But it's not cool to use your kid to make money busking. You know that, right, Donny?"

"You've got it wrong, Norb," Donny said. "I had no choice. Anyway, Stewart loves it when I busk. He loves the attention. He's a real people person. Just like his dad. A chip off the old block."

"Thank God he got Allison's looks," Tony said. His mouth was grim. I could tell he was mad that Donny had brought his kid into this mess. Tony is prickly, but he's a real good dad.

"Low blow, Tony," Donny said, as he inhaled his cruller.

"So what's up, Love?" Tony said, gesturing at the guitar. "Attention-seeking, *again*? I thought you got over that, after last year."

"What? A man can't dream again? Do you know how long I've wanted to perform one of my original tunes live? And now I've finally found the courage to do it. So you guys should be encouraging me, not scolding me." He turned his laser beam on me. "You're a writer, Norb, you get me, right?" His intensity was almost frightening.

"Yeah, Donny," Tony said, "you always have the courage to be an idiot. Good for you. What did you do this time? Get fired?"

"What? No! Of course not! But I need more. I have a creative spirit."

"Of course, Donny, I get it," I said, finally, "but I don't have time to discuss that right now. I need you to help me with something really important."

"Like what?" he asked. He slugged back some coffee. He was still wearing his Village Idiots jersey.

"First things first," Tony said, shutting me down. "What the frig is with the billboard at Flux and Steel, Love? You're a fiction writer, now? Selling a book called *Making Steven Famous* written by Dave Walker? As in, the kid from Grade Nine Shop Class? Please tell me you didn't, *tell* me you didn't."

Donny avoided Tony's gaze. Tony jerked his middle finger at Donny's face then threw his hands up in the air. "Fucking hot dog, I knew it. Here we go again."

"Wasn't Dave Walker the skinny, geeky kid with the aviator glasses?" John said. His brow furrowed. "What kind of boring pseudonym is that? Might as well have called yourself John Doe or Bill White."

"I remember that kid," Tony said. "He would screw with your head, then rubber-band away like Elastic Man. He was annoying."

"Donny," I said, changing the subject, "as an author, I'm telling you you can't use Dave Walker's name as a pseudonym for your self-published book. You realize that's totally illegal, right?" I searched the other's faces for approval, but they were too busy staring at Donny as if deciding if now would be a good time to hog-tie him and drive him to the psych ward.

Donny was pumping his leg. "Walker deserves to be famous, man, just like Steven does. Walker was inspirational. He was a Super Ball. You'd chuck him against the sidewalk and he'd bounce back a different guy with a new idea or a plan, or a, a powerful life philosophy. Plus, he was also the ultimate Elastic Man. Remember that? And, despite being a skinny nerd, he never backed down from a fight. Probably why he ended up dead. At least that's what Westerbrook told me. You guys wouldn't believe half the stories I've unearthed about him. He was a chameleon! Apparently, he skipped classes one afternoon in Grade Eleven and snuck into the Blue Ball, got hammered and started mouthing off to some bikers, so they stuck a shiv in his head. So, as far as I can tell, his name's totally up for grabs. Plus, it's a common name, so legally anyone can use it." A sadness fell across Donny's face. "I had a lot of respect for Walker."

"I guess he was like that, wasn't he," Tony said, stroking his chin, suddenly deep in thought. "Always playing with fire. Lipped off to bikers, huh? Doesn't fucking surprise me. What a fucking lunatic. Took a page right out of your playbook, Love."

Donny looked like he was surfing the manic waves inside his brain.

"Are you *sure* Walker's dead, Donny?" John said. "We all thought Steven was dead and we know how wrong we were about that."

Donny looked at us. "Look, guys, I don't know why you've got your knickers in a knot about this. I wrote a book about us searching for Steven. It needed to be told. It's our story. As the saying goes, write what you know. This will be a hit. A *guaran-fucking-teed hit!*" His eyes grew even wider, if such a thing were possible.

"How much did all of that cost you?" I asked. "The self-publishing, the billboard? I mean most self-published authors don't recoup their money. That's a known fact." I knew this 'cause I'd looked into it, many times.

Donny shrugged. "Four grand, chump change. I'll recoup that in no time. As we speak, I'm selling the book on Lulu and Amazon and my website. It's all-a-go, Daddy-O."

"Does Allison know?" Tony asked. "Cause you remember how you just about destroyed your marriage the same way about, oh, nine or ten months ago?"

Donny gulped. "Fuck off. That's really none of your business."

"Poor Allison," I said. "And Stewart, too."

Stewart was fidgeting in his chair. Donny gave him his soo-soo and he began sucking on it, arching backwards to take in his surroundings.

"Look, man, just stick with your *In Town* column," John said. "*That* pays the bills. And keeps Allison happy. And instead of blowing four grand on another scheme, you could have used that money to set up an RESP for your kid."

Donny leaned over and patted John on the cheek. "Oh, Sweet Johnny Pappas. Ye of little faith. I'll make way more money than that. And I'll sock all of it way in a killer trust fund. It's all about believing in yourself."

Tony leaned forward into Donny's personal space. He was really mad—a familiar expression—but I thought he looked queasy, too. "You, Donny Love, are batshit crazy. You wrote a book about *us* and now you're hawking it under a fake name that's actually a real name? Only someone completely insane or completely selfish would stoop so friggin' low. Do you *never* learn from your experiences?" He grasped to find words. "You are beyond the pale, Donny. End of fucking story." He turned to Stewart. "Sorry, Stewart, bad word. Don't ever say that one." He patted the little guy's head.

Mr. Tell-it-like-it-is, I thought.

My timing was lousy, but I couldn't afford to waste another moment. "Donny, will *you* help me?"

"Help?" Donny repeated, vaguely. His eyes had glazed over. I could tell from experience he was deep into the rabbit hole of his latest scheme. It could take hours for him to pull out of it.

I explained, yet again.

"The Screw?" he said. He blinked, and shook his head. He was back into our world. His eyes shifted, like he was watching gyrating pinwheels. "Awesome character name, Norb. Do you mind if I use it in my next book? I'll give you five percent royalties on every sale."

My anger skyrocketed. "What the fuzz?! I just told you The Screw is on the verge of murdering my family and all you care about is using his name in your next book?" I clenched my fists. "Five percent royalties? Royalties from *what*, you nutbar stinkerhead!"

Despite being really furious with Donny, I felt a sudden and unwanted pang of empathy for my old friend. I threw myself back in my chair. Donny's mental health was obviously a mess, and, although I was ashamed to admit it, there were times when my own mental health had been pretty fragile. Only last year, I'd mugged for the tv cameras in Mutti's basement, half-lying about my close friendship with Steven, banging my drum set like a toddler; and I'd spent years trying to find fame as a comic book artist, although I swear that most of the time I did it for the art. I hadn't seen Donny this manic since he'd staged last year's Steven Dundee come back concert. Maybe Donny really did need medication. Maybe none of what Donny did was his fault.

"We should place an anonymous call to some drug dealers and tell them The Screw is muscling in on their territory," Tony said. "Maybe they'd kidnap him and dump him into the Bay wearing a pair of size fourteen lead boots."

Tony just shrugged when everyone stared blank-faced at him, and after that there was a lot of lip-biting and deep sighing and single eyebrow raising. Tony made a fist with one arm, and slapped his upper arm with his other hand—his trademark *ombrello* gesture.

"Oh my Gawd!" Donny gasped, ducking down. "It's them!"

"Who?" Tony said, following Donny's gaze. "All I see is two teenagers leaving a black Smart Car and heading for Canadian Tire." He threw John and me a look.

"Smith and Smith," Donny said. "They're after me, *again*. They must have seen the billboard. I bet Walker's hired a lawyer to sue me. Or maybe it has something to do with the time I dressed up as Dolly Parton and paraded around the mall. My Incognito group warned me about trying that. And they're never wrong. Fucking mall security booted me out." He tapped his head with his index finger. "I bet they reported me to the cops and Smith and Smith got wind of it." He was breathing rapidly.

What the fuzz? Why couldn't my friends just focus on my life-or-death pickle? It was like they all had ADHD. I watched, stunned, as he dove under the table.

"Are you fucking serious?" Tony said. "Get out from under there!" He looked embarrassed.

The ladies at the table next to us were eyeing us suspiciously. Elise was narrowing her eyes.

Donny whispered from under the table. "I saw them getting out of their car. Can't you see them, Tony? Dark suits? Dark sunglasses?"

Tony looked like he wanted to take a carburetor to Donny's head.

"Hmph. I don't see anyone," John said. He looked down at Donny as if he was a toad. "We haven't seen Smith and Smith since last year. If your delusions persist, I *strongly* suggest a visit to Dr. Ceroni."

Everyone I knew went to our G.P., Dr. Ceroni. I'd been going to him since I was born. He was well into his eighties. His office was next to Super Affordable Cremation & Burial Services, across the street from the bowling alley. The thing is, I wasn't too sure the old guy would have a clue what to do with Donny Love.

"Since when are *you* a shrink, John?" Tony said. "Are you ditching the restaurant business? Maybe you can set up an office in Norb's comic book shop. Tons of nut jobs show up there. You'll get rich in no freakin' time." He avoided looking at Donny and shook his head angrily.

John bristled. "Or I could set up shop in your repair bay, Tony. Drive-by psychotherapist, Dr. John Pappas." He winked at Tony. "And for you, my friend, the initial assessment is on the house."

"How about I bury *you* under a house," Tony said.

Stewart started bawling. Without missing a beat, Donny reached up and re-inserted his son's soo-soo. Unbelievably, Stewart accepted it and once again was content to listen and watch.

Out of the blue, it struck me that I was on my own. My fuzzin' friends couldn't or wouldn't accept The Screw was real. I wasn't even a priority for them. They weren't taking me seriously, and never had, not really.

Deep down, I knew it was up to me alone to fight an evil small, creepy dwarf with a googly eye, huge feet, and a shiny gun.

Out of the corner of my eye, something caught my attention. I found myself staring past the counter to the take-out window. Poking above it was a black fedora trimmed with a red ribbon, the same one The Screw had worn at ComWorld! The driver's window slid down, and a large beefy hand reached up and accepted an extra-large coffee. I heard myself make an unmanly squeak.

"Norb, did you get that awesome email I sent you?" Donny said conversationally, from under the table.

"Oh my Gawd," I screamed, my voice returning. "It's The Screw!"

For a split second, everything went deadly quiet.

Chapter 6

Half-asleep, a headache pounding in my skull, I shut our apartment door and shuffled down the steep stairs leading to the back door of our shop.

Last night, after seeing The Screw at the Tim's drive-thru and enduring my friends' crappy ambivalence, I'd been unable to sleep. I'd spent most of the night guzzling Jolt Cola and patrolling the Village on my Vespa. I don't know what I actually could have done if The Screw *had* shown up. Run him over? Who was I kidding?

I'd fought the urge to go to Mutti's basement, grab Dad's Luger, and cradle it across my lap like the Terminator. But if I shot The Screw first, assuming I had the courage *and* the skill, I'd end up in jail, and that would be a worse fate than an eternity in hell with Donny, or John for that matter. Because it would be a life without Morag.

Memories of Donny's nonsense at the coffee shop irked me, waking me up the rest of the way. Although I wasn't exactly the poster child for maturity, Donny had barely grown up.

When Morag and I have a baby, no fuzzin' way am I going to be anything like Donny. I'm going to be a better dad. But then I felt another pang for him, as I always did, and I hated that I did, because he mostly didn't deserve a pang from anyone.

I stopped before opening the shop door. I remembered what Donny had asked me while cowering under the table at Tim's. "*Norb, did you get that awesome email I sent you?*"

He regularly sent me links to his songs on Bandcamp, and I'd reluctantly have a listen. The music itself was pretty good, but, sadly, his voice sucked. I didn't have the heart to tell him. He tried so hard to sing, it was painful to witness.

"Awesome email?" I said out loud. "I highly doubt it, Donny." But sometimes Donny sent me links to funny memes and, at that moment, in the face of everything bad that was happening in my life, I really needed a ton of funny. I turned on my new iPhone, which I'd been waiting months for, like the tech nerd that I was, and found Donny's link.

Big fuzzin' mistake!

Blood drained from my face. The landing at the bottom of the stairs elongated in my mind like an airport runway. I landed on my bum on the bottom step.

I was watching a YouTube video titled "Humpty Dumpty, the Village Vigilante". Donny grinned in his profile picture. Over one million views! *Oh my gawd! This video has gone viral!* The video was footage of me from Saturday night bursting out the front doors of Mutti's house and chasing The Screw's car down Steel Street, wearing, of all things, *Morag's red leggings!* Someone had filmed me on their phone and uploaded it! *Donny? How the fuck did you get this?* The soundtrack to the video was Donny's "Stompin' Tom Connors" song from his Bandcamp page, but the idiot had changed the words, and for once he actually sounded not half-bad! Now the chorus was:

"They call him Humpty Dumpty
He's big and he's round
And he'll protect your town
They call him Humpty Dumpty"

Donny had tracked in hip hop rhythms and scratch sound effects, stuttering the footage in sync with the various rhythms. I juddered back and forth across the screen, and so did The Screw's car. I would have laughed my arse off, if I hadn't been so angry and embarrassed and scared, and—shocked. *Christ, I really do look like Humpty Dumpty from the chip bag.* I was scared because I really didn't know how The Screw would react if he saw this video. Did evil dwarves watch YouTube? Was that a thing?

But *if* the universe had birthed me with a big head, and *if* that was a bad thing—Morag always said it definitely wasn't—it was *Donny* who'd used my big head for his own gain, without asking for permission. That was my crazy friend's M.O. And now, thanks to him, I looked like some kind of crazy freak myself, on the internet, where millions of people could see me. *But I'm not a fuzzin' freak! Or a criminal! I'm Norbert Reingruber! Humble comic book shop owner and married man! Donny, you stupid, selfish bastard, how could you do this to me?!*

I clicked on the comments, knowing it would be a mistake.

One guy wrote, "Finally, someone with the balls to rid the scum from our neighbourhoods, cops are friggin' useless, go Humpty!" *I'm not a vigilante!* Gene Simmons wrote, "Humpty Dumpty, they make the best chips, you rock Humpty!" Wait? *the* Gene Simmons from *Kiss?* Someone named Mark Smiley wrote: "What an ugly bastard, only a mother could love that freak!" *That's really mean, Mark."* Mike Myers responded, "Man for a guy that size, he can really run." *I can? Is this the real Mike Myers, the comedian? Is he kidding or being serious?* Someone named Candy-O wrote, "I always knew Humpty was a superhero in disguise!" *I'm no fuzzin superhero, Cars fan! and I'm not Humpty fuzzin' Dumpty.* Another guy wrote, "Love the tights Norbie, message me for a good time, no strings attached, you'll be in and out in no time." *In and out? Yikes! No thanks, buddy!*

I turned off the video, feeling queasy. "What have you done to me, Donny? You corksucking, son of a bum!"

Tentatively, I opened the back door to Steel Town Comics, expecting to see the real Humpty standing there driving a fist at my face for stealing the limelight. I had to find a way out of this situation fast. My head spun with conflicting possibilities.

Instead of finding Humpty, I found Tank and Harlan and Morag. Somehow they hadn't heard me yelling. I was so relieved. I didn't want them to think I was crazy.

Like clockwork, Morag had brought a tray of coffees and a bag of donuts for us comic book evangelists, her Monday morning ritual before crossing the street to work at the Irondale Library. I was suddenly ravenous. My thinking was always razor sharp on a full stomach, especially a stomach lovingly filled with sweets and caffeine. I hurried over and helped myself.

Morag was sipping coffee, chatting with Tank Girl about her cat's urinary tract problems. Tank Girl's real name was Mary Blithe; she was in her early twenties, tall and gangly. She hated being called Mary, but was okay with Tank. She wore scuffed black army boots, the same colour as almost everything else she wore. Both sides of her head were shaved, and a shock of dyed red hair swooped out the side of the green army helmet she wore when she was in battle mode, which was most of the time. She didn't suffer fools lightly, and had once physically bounced a punk customer for announcing to a packed store that the real Tank Girl was a total *wuss* and couldn't fight her way out of a paper bag. That was his first and last mistake. He never came back to the shop, ever.

"Norb," Harlan said, urgently, staring at the computer. "I'm taking tomorrow off. You're cool with that, right? Thanks, Norb. You're the man."

Harlan had thick brown hair, parted at the side, and always wore collared shirts and dress pants from Sears. A pair of light brown boat shoes stuck out from the cuffs of his beige pants. He was in his mid-forties, and, like Tank, worked part-time at the shop. Harlan didn't look like a comic book nerd. In fact, he looked like a Mormon.

"Uh, I am?" I said. *Tuesdays are Tank's day off. Who will mind the store?* I caught Morag giving me the stink eye, and quickly glanced away. She hated it when I caved to Harlan's and Tank's last-minute demands. Her words from last week drifted through my head. "*They want to respect you, Norbie. But they can't because you're a pushover. Show them who's boss, okay?*" She'd said to me, time and time again, that I needed to create a sick day and vacation request policy, and then give it to my staff, explain it, and enforce it regularly. I knew she was right, but, like so many other things in my life, I just hadn't gotten around to it yet. Back in high school, I'd handed in all my school assignments late, but somehow I'd graduated. If I'd handed my stuff in on time, I probably could have become a brain surgeon, or an x-ray technician at the very least. Morag said that if I managed Harlan and Tank properly, and wasn't always covering their shifts for them, then that would free up more time for me to *run* the business, rather than working *in* the business.

Morag was right, of course. She was now a part-time branch manager at the Irondale Library, and had taken all the city-offered management courses, so she knew what the heck she was talking about. I thought I was ready to try her methods, but first I had to figure out how to handle potential conflict from my staff. I really had to get past my desperate need to be liked.

The first step would be to call Donny and order him to pull the You Tube video! *Do it, Norb!*

I will, I yelled at the voice inside me head, *just let me wake up first!*

"Check this out," Harlan said. He'd connected his iPod to the old Sears stereo behind the counter. "New Army of Darkness tune, "'Chainsaw and Sorcery'", based of course on the awesome comic book series and the best horror movie ever fuckin' made. And, of course, corporate radio will never play this, but I sure as fuck will. Right, Tank Girl? We know how much you *love* the corporations."

Heavy metal music blasted out the speakers.

I was only half-listening—all I could think about was Humpty Dumpty stutter-stepping down Steel Street in Donny's viral YouTube video. It was beyond ludicrous. Had Donny inadvertently blown The Screw's cover? Was he now on his way kill us, ahead of schedule?

As soon as I guzzled my coffee and scarfed a jelly donut, I vowed to call Donny and order him to pull the video. Then the books needed to be pulled, and *fast*.

Last Christmas, Harlan had mounted extra speakers in the ceiling corners. He hadn't asked my permission, but I hadn't minded. Like him, I loved my music loud. I saw the best in Harlan, even if Morag and Tank didn't. Morag said he was a know-it-all, and Tank's feelings about Harlan were written all over her face. Especially when his old-man music assaulted her young, space-age ears.

Morag and Tank glared at Harlan. Finally, Tank said. "Your tastes are so antiquated Harlan. And don't even try converting me to your archaic music."

Harlan scoffed. "Gee, sorry I didn't enjoy "'Suicide Landscape'" and the rest of your cheery goth tunes. Next time I want to kill myself, I'll be sure and give them a spin." He didn't even crack a smile.

Harlan and Tank always started the day hating on each other. Tank was definitely sharper than Harlan when it came to the underground comic scene, but Harlan knew more about comics in general. He was the shop historian. Harlan knew a ton about old school comics, and, other than his last-minute time-off demands, he was a huge asset. He had the gift of the gab and knew exactly how to chat up the nerdiest of comic book fans, especially the older ones. Tank sometimes intimidated the parental customer, but she was a total rockstar with the younger crowd, and they often showed up just to be seen hanging out with her.

Harlan was our shop website builder and webmaster. He'd made it look really good, although he kept putting off adding in the shopping cart feature, refusing to give the processing company a penny of *our* money. Personally, I think it had less to do with saving the business money than Harlan's hatred of the corporate robber Barons. I'd been meaning to talk to him about that, but kept putting it off. Luckily, in-store customers usually sought his advice and bought books and merch on impulse, so that helped pay the rent and keep the shop from going under.

Morag whispered into my ear, "Norbie, tell Harlan he *must* work tomorrow, tell him you need to drive Mutti to the hospital. Tell him that from now on he has to give you a week's notice to book time off. And please tell him to turn down the music. It's way too loud."

I nodded. Once again, I tried really hard to follow Morag's advice, but this time I'd mostly been thinking about how I needed to contact Donny to make sure he shut down my video before it went supernova. I guzzled coffee to avoid taking action.

"I will." I set my mouth in a grim line. "I'll do it soon." I knew she didn't believe me. *I* didn't believe me.

"Babe, it'll bother your customers."

Morag's voice echoed inside my head. *What customers?* I thought.

With so much online competition and computer games grabbing kids' attentions, comic book sales had slowed dramatically. Fewer customers showed up at the shop. I'd barely made the last rent payment—I'd had to throw in fifty bucks in quarters I'd saved up in a pickle jar under the bed. Two months earlier, desperate to stay open and keep doing what I loved, I'd asked the landlord to do a reno to reduce the floor space, and he'd agreed. Now, our shop was the size of a shoebox, but at least I could *almost* pay the rent and the wages of two part-time employees. If not for Morag's solid city job, we'd still be living in Mutti's basement. I knew I needed to have "the discussion", as Morag liked to put it, with Tank about reducing her hours. But what if she got mad at me? What if she started crying? Geez, I already felt so bad for her. Like me, she'd finally moved out of her parents' house, (*eighteen years earlier than you did, loser),* and she had rent to pay like a real adult. I really didn't think I could give her the bad news. Someone else would have to. I'd get Harlan to do it. Well, that would definitely start World War III. I sighed. *Man up, Norb!* I really hoped for everyone's sake that sales improved soon.

Instead of discussing my expectations with Harlan and denying him his time off, or contacting Donny to pull down the video, or actively removing *The Steeltown Avenger* from bookshelves across the

U.S. of A., I did zero constructive stuff. Instead, I plopped down on the stool beside Harlan, fired up my laptop, and surfed the internet.

Surfing always helped me find distraction from my problems. Courtesy of the MegaFreak website and Ebay, tons of collectables and memorabilia were stored in my basement shrine at Mutti's. Lately, I'd been searching for a cool KISS belt buckle.

But then I made a serious blunder. I looked up. Morag was glaring at me. Today, she was wearing her pink Wonder Woman t-shirt. I could barely resist her. For a mortal, she has a lot of power. She jerked her head toward Harlan.

"Okay," I mouthed.

I cleared my throat, and somehow gathered up my courage. "Harlan, how come you need the day off?"

"How did ComWorld go, Norbie?" he asked, smoothly, ignoring my question. He's so good, that guy. "Did you sign any autographs?"

"Yeah, Norb," said Tank, "did you kill it?"

"I don't think so," I said, staring back at my computer screen. I was not off to a good start.

"Why not?" Tank asked.

"Harlan?" I said a bit louder. "I asked you a question." I gulped. *Gawd, I hate being the bad guy. I'm just not cut out to be a manager.*

Harlan shrugged me off and answered his ringing cell phone rang. "... Yes, Val, I spoke to the lawyer. Yes, I'll put our bank account in your name. I'll give you the keys tomorrow. Yes, I'll go with you to see the lawyer. I know it's the last time, and yes, I'll be there." He hung up and stared at me. He squeezed his phone so tightly I thought it would shatter.

"My ex is killing me, Norb. She left me for a fucking eye doctor, who's not only loaded but he's also an egotistical dick, and somehow, with the help of her fancy lawyer, *she* gets the fucking house and the car." Tears formed behind his eyes. "Can you fucking believe that, Norbie?"

"I'm so sorry, Harlan."

He lowered his voice. "And now I'm living in a shit-hole basement apartment I'm renting from some Hell's Angel named Lou." He took a deep breath. "So, while my ex is living the good life in cosy Ancaster, I'm living across from Dofasco in fucking Mordor!"

I saw the pain and hurt in Harlan's eyes. I felt so bad for him.

"At least I have a job," he said, quietly, "even if it's only part-time." He shifted his gaze to Tank. "Even if I have to work with some punk know-it-all named *Tank*."

Tank stuck her tongue out at him, but I could tell she was holding back. Usually she also gives him the finger.

Rolling his eyes, he glanced back at me. "What were you asking me, Norb?"

My mind blanked. I'd felt so bad for him I forgot that I'd asked him why he needed a day off. "I, uh, just wanted to say good luck on your day off."

"Luck?" Harlan grumbled, ripping open a courier package. "Lady Luck has left the station, my friend, with Doctor Asshole."

A wall went down behind Morag's eyes. I'd seen that wall a thousand times when I'd disappointed her, mostly because of my procrastination. Morag was right—although it was okay for me to feel sorry for Harlan, it wasn't okay for me accept his last-minute insistence on time off. All I had to do, I told myself, was deliver my expectations to Harlan in a sensitive and caring manner and then it would be over. So what was the big deal? Why was I so afraid to do that?

Morag finished her coffee, said a curt goodbye to everyone, and headed out of the shop to go to work.

"Morag, wait!"

Pain jerked my heartstrings.

I couldn't handle it when Morag was mad at me, not that I blamed her, but what I really couldn't handle was thinking her heart had hardcore hardened towards me. I'd rather die than have that happen.

The door swung shut behind her.

I was paralyzed with fear and sadness.

Guilt gnawed away at me. In the past, Morag had given me tons of chances *not* to procrastinate, but each and every time I'd let her down. I almost hated myself for it. *Grow a pair, Norb!*

"Harlan," I said, straightening my spine, "mind if we talk?"

He was deep into his own head and hadn't heard me. Or had he?

"The print quality of these new comic books is atrocious," he said, flipping a page.

I cleared my throat. "Harlan, did you hear what I said?" I was trembling now, afraid that Harlan would get mad at me.

"I'm listening, Norb."

I gathered up my courage. *Do this for Morag!* I surprised myself and cut to the chase. "Harlan, about tomorrow, you can't just take a day off whenever you want, you need to—"

My phone rang. I saw that it was Mutti. *Not now, Mutti! I've finally found the courage to deal with Harlan!* If not for her cancer condition, I would have let her call go to voice mail.

"Mutti," I said so loudly I scared myself.

Harlan shrugged me off and went to help Tank shelve new inventory.

As I listened to my mother, my heart was a hot coal in my chest. "I'll be right there!"

I hung up. "Harlan, close up the store today without me!"

"Can't," Harlan said. He turned up his music. "I was going to leave early today. I have to see my lawyer. Get Tank to close."

She threw him a dirty look.

My face filled with hot blood. "I don't care who closes, Harlan, you fucking misanthrope! Work it out with Tank! And turn down that fucking music! It'll scare away customers and we barely have any!"

I didn't care that I'd sworn. But I felt bad calling Harlan a misanthrope.

Harlan's jaw had dropped. By the look on his face, I'd suddenly transformed into the Incredible Hulk.

I barely wondered what Tank and Harlan were thinking, as they watched their boss, Norbert Reingruber, aka The Village Vigilante/ Humpty Dumpty, fly awkwardly out of the store, tears streaming down his cheeks, his heart breaking into a million pieces.

Chapter 7

I'D NO SOONER STUMBLED out the door, when it seemed that people were moving towards me. A second later I realized what was happening. *The paparazzi? You've got to be fuzzin' kidding me!* There was a Channel 11 news truck and a white CKOC van stamped with red letters on its side panel. Channel 11 had a cameraman and a female reporter with a microphone. CKOC had a scruffy old guy with a tape recorder. Both of them moved fast.

They both asked me stuff. I may have answered some questions, but I was too amped up and single-minded to remember my answers later on. Crazy questions about Steven Dundee. Was I still his best childhood friend? And did I still play drums? Was I in touch with John and Tony? Had we found the real Steven? Was he still engaging in selfless acts of heroism in distant countries? Saving lives in Afghanistan? Had he returned to acting and singing? Was he in touch with Maurice? And then the worst questions of all. How was my new life as a vigilante? Was I working with CSIS? How many criminals had I foiled? Did I fear for my life? Could they interview me working in my shop so they could work the hometown boy angle? Stuff like that.

Next door, Jimmy-the-Barber—the same barber from the same Scottish mining town as Donny's dad's—was outside his shop taking a smoke break. A cigarette dangled from his lower lip as he chewed one of the gum balls from his gum ball machine. He'd been cutting my hair since I was three. "Norbie, you okay, lad? Want me to put the run on these eejits?" I opened my mouth to tell him not to worry, but all that came out was a confused-sounding squeak. Typical.

"The bloody media," Jimmy said, "bunch of boggin' parasites." If they heard him, they didn't react.

A City TV truck skidded onto the tarmac strip fronting the shops and out popped another reporter and cameraman; a CBC van jumped the curb at the same time a Hamilton Gazette reporter flew out of a hard-braking taxi. Somehow, the Channel 11 cameraman had found a way to work his camera while also drinking a coffee and smoking a cig.

I was blocked in. It was like that time in Grade Nine when I stupidly took Tony's advice to try out for Junior Football and just about had a panic attack during a pile-on. Microphones danced in front of my eyes. Reporters hurled questions at me. I was so stressed out I couldn't decipher one question from the next.

Desperate to escape, I pulled what would later be described as a *Humpty Dumpty*.

I sprinted, knowing I'd be super-fast for one-hundred metres before gassing out. I'd be far enough away from the cameras to boot the rest of the way to Mutti's house before they caught up to me.

After running out of steam on Flux Road, south of the Village intersection, I glanced over my shoulder and saw media vehicles charging along the road towards me. Heart racing, I staggered along the sidewalk towards Mutti's house, like a Humpty Dumpty chip bag blown by a hard, unforgiving wind.

Chapter 8

AT NOON, MORAG AND I were sitting in chairs beside Mutti's bed at Henderson Hospital. Morag hadn't said a word since arriving—she was too choked up. Gently, she stroked Mutti's hair. My mother was unconscious.

In the tight little cubicle in the E.R., Mutti was hooked up to complicated machines blinking red light and several IV bags. Seeing her so vulnerable knifed my heart.

My mind was reeling. Hopefully, the Doctor would tell us a big mistake had been made, that Mutti's hemorrhage was what? A minor setback? Hardly.

I'd found Mutti curled up in a ball on the kitchen floor, clutching her abdomen, groaning in pain. I'd almost fainted at the sight of all the blood soaking her pants. I must have gone into a state of shock because I couldn't remember calling 911. Once I knew Mutti was safe in an emergency room bed, I'd stumbled past the nurse's station, found a bathroom, and barfed into the toilet. Afterwards, I'd called Morag and she'd come right away.

I'd almost cried with relief when I saw my wife speed down the hall toward me. She was my knight in shining armour, man. She hugged me tightly, and nothing ever felt so good.

"Oh! Karl!" I said.

"Don't worry," Morag said. "I've already called him. Just focus on Mutti, OK?"

The PA system was buzzing with announcements. Through a large gap in the cubicle drapes, I'd been watching paramedics wheeling in patients, and nurses and Doctors conferencing. In the next bed, a man was groaning loudly. I figured his pain meds had worn off.

After a while, I couldn't handle thinking about Mutti, so I punished myself by thinking about Donny. *I'm not a fuzzin' Our Town vigilante, and I'm not fuzzin' Humpty Dumpty! You know, it's pretty insulting to call someone Humpty Dumpty. I think the term is fat-shaming! Donny, you better have a good fuzzin' reason for lying to the world about me!*

I exhaled, slowly.

I tried to swallow the huge lump in my throat as I held Mutti's hand. She was terribly pale. Her breathing was shallow. I barely recognized her, and that broke my heart even more. After about twenty minutes of waiting, a doctor came in and closed the curtains behind her.

She was a slight woman with sandy blonde hair. Her brown eyes were intelligent, magnified behind a pair of thick-lensed glasses in soft pink frames. She wore a Mickey Mouse surgeon's cap, which made me feel better, oddly enough.

"Hello. I'm Dr. Khan. I—"

I jolted up into a standing position. "My mother said everything was going to be okay," I blurted. "She was scheduled to have surgery tomorrow. What the heck's going on here?" My heart was racing.

Morag trained her eyes on the surgeon. "This is Norbert Reingruber," she said to the doctor. "Anna's son."

The surgeon nodded and faced me. "Norbert, your mom's lucky to be alive, considering the amount of blood loss. Good thing you got her here when you did."

"Lucky to be alive?" I shot a glance from Morag back to the doctor. "Tomorrow she's supposed to go in for a routine operation, and now you say she's lucky to be alive? None of that makes sense to me." I was almost hyperventilating.

"We're going to top your mom up with a transfusion before I perform emergency surgery. I *will* remove the tumour."

"But I thought her tumour wasn't that serious. I thought she was going to have it removed and everything would go back to normal." *Is this really happening?*

Dr. Khan sighed. "Unfortunately, it's more than just a tumour." She paused. "I'm guessing your mom never discussed the details with you."

"No, I guess she didn't." *You're always trying to protect me Mutti. Ever since I was a little boy. And I used to get mad at you when you did that. I'm sorry I gave you a hard time Mutti, I really am.* I was on the verge of bawling.

"Even with the latest MRI, I can't see exactly what's going on until I perform surgery. From experience, I can say that when a woman hemorrhages the way your mother did, there's something else going on. It's quite possible the cancer has spread to the surrounding tissue."

Morag squeezed my hand. I avoided her gaze. *Please, God, tell me this isn't happening.*

Dr. Khan continued: "Right now your mom's feeling no pain and that's a very good thing. The surgery takes two to three hours. I'll find you in the waiting area afterwards. Hang in there. Stay strong for your mom."

"Thanks so much, Doctor," Morag said.

I nodded numbly, as the doctor disappeared through the curtains.

Suddenly, the reek of disinfectant was making me squeamish. And seeing all these sick lonely people was way too much for my already burdened heart. Dad had been so lucky—he'd died of a sudden heart attack and missed the misery of the hospital. *Everyone gets their turn,* his voice echoed inside my head. As a kid, I remembered him saying that to Mutti, but only now did I realize the truth of his words.

Why did anyone have to die? It just felt so completely *wrong.*

Morag was eyeing me empathetically. Her mom had died ten years earlier of breast cancer, so she knew what I was going through. Seeing the woman I loved so much standing by me as Mutti was—*dying?*—finally cleaved me open. I began crying, softly, punctuated by an occasional peeping sound that only someone like me can make.

Morag hugged me. "Don't worry, Norbie. Mutti would hate it if she knew you were worrying about her. That's why she downplayed the seriousness of her tumour."

"She shouldn't have done that. I'm a grown man, Morag. I can handle the truth."

No, I can't, not really.

"I know you can," she whispered. She hugged me closer. "Just know that Mutti really loves you."

Pawing away my tears, I rested my head on Morag's shoulder, but then I froze in horror. The Screw slipped through the gap in the drapes, followed by his two thugs, twice his size and uglier.

His stoved-in face guzzled the fluorescent light. He was horrifying to look at, a Cyclops, his gammy, googly eye scanning the room. He tilted his fedora at Morag, then leered at her breasts. She flicked a glance at me and I nodded. *This is the creep I've been telling you about, and yeah Morag my love, he's fuzzin' real. Shit's going down.*

She gripped the bed rail, knuckles blanching.

"I saw your friend's dumb YouTube video," The Screw said, "and the other five that nutcase pumped out in the last hour. One of them stupidly shows Humpty Dumpty chasing me in my car. Over a million views. *Of me.*" His eyes narrowed. "What's that asshole's problem? Huh, Norbie? Does he have a serious death wish?"

I nodded.

My heart was hammering in my chest. Five more videos? What the hell Donny? Oh-frickin'-frackin' fuzz. *Is The Screw really standing at the foot of Mutti's hospital bed?*

He inched closer to me. "If Love doesn't shut down those videos in sixty minutes, tomorrow's deadline doesn't exist. And everyone dies yesterday."

He glared down at Mutti. He scoffed. "Mutti? What kind of fucking Kraut name is that?"

My stomach curdled.

Flames shot out of Morag's eyes.

The Screw scowled at me. "Shadow's not only a powerful man, he's a secretive man, and he doesn't want any fucking arrows pointing his way, especially not a bunch of warped nerd arrows generated from bullshit videos." His bad eye puckered in its socket. He looked like he wanted to spit.

"Okay," I said, finally, my voice super trembly, "I'll call Donny." *How could you possibly know I call my mom Mutti? Are you bugging her house? Are you bugging my apartment? My store? Or did that bumhead Donny tell you?* The Screw knew way too much about me and my friends. How did he know all this?

He leered at Morag's breasts again then looked back at me. "Is any of this making sense to you, Norbie?"

He tapped his watch. "Well, then get moving. Tick, tock, tick, tock."

I was pulling out my iPhone, scrolling for Donny in my contacts, when The Screw winked lustfully at Morag, and that turned her expression murderous. I barely recognized her. He tore open his trench coat and revealed a shiny revolver sticking out of his belt. "How do you like my pistol, baby? Same size as my shoes, *if* you get my drift." He laughed like a greasy pervert and tapped his long, skinny dress shoe against the floor. "Once you go Screw, Norbie will just not do." He laughed lustfully. So did his thugs.

Morag bolted up from her seat, her eyes blazing with fury, her fists cocked, when an orderly wheeled in a stretcher to take Mutti to surgery. She didn't complete the swing, but there was a moment when I thought she really would.

I'd never seen her that boiling mad, and that was really saying something. I mean, she *is* a redhead.

The Screw tipped his hat at the orderly and spun out of the room like an errant bowling ball, his thugs spinning after him. The orderly looked dazed.

Shaking with fear, rage, and uncertainty, I couldn't decide if I should stay put with Morag at the hospital, or call Donny and order him to shut down the videos, or make a mad dash to his house, confront him in person, and actually watch him shut down the videos so I'd know he actually had and wasn't *lying* that he had. Or should I call hospital security and tell them how a psychotic evil dwarf had just threatened us? Or call the police and press charges against The Screw? Or chase him and do what? Fight him? And his thugs? They'd cream me, for sure.

Fear and anger had really paralyzed me.

I didn't know which way to turn.

Chapter 9

"SNAP OUT OF IT NORB!"

Morag's voice snapped me out of my paralysis. She grabbed my hand, and we booted after the orderly wheeling Mutti onto the open elevator.

I phoned Tye Novak, determined to straighten out my mess once and for all. But before I could utter a single word, he cried, "Norbie! My number one writer! I—"

"Tye, haul my books out of all the shops! Now! My family and I are about to die!...What? Look, I don't care if we're going to get rich, and I don't need to be famous."

I was talking to Tye with real authority—I'd never talked to *anyone* that way before. "I've told you, Tye, The Screw is freakin' real. Listen, I'll re-write the book and make up a device similar to the Invisiblator and then we'll make so much money you and Alex can buy a yacht and sail the world! Okay? How awesome would that be?...What? My next book? How does that work, Tye? Cause if *The Steeltown Avenger* stays on the shelves, Morag and I will be dead, so who's going to write it, or any other book in the series? Tye, you realize you'll make tons more money if I'm *not dead*, right?...Are you fuzzin' serious?"

I wanted to reach through the phone and slap him. "Please Tye, I'm begging you, for my family's sake, pull the books!...One-hundred and fourteen stores? Are you shitting me? How is that possible? Tye?" He'd hung up.

I stared at my phone numbly. It dawned on me that I might actually become famous. Probably posthumously. I just wanted to be safe and happy and barely solvent, tucked away in the Village, in the Hammer, with my family and my idiot friends.

And I realized now it was totally impossible for me or anyone else to go down to the U.S. and remove so many books from so many stores. The logistics would be insanely complicated. The cost would be astronomical. I was royally screwed. Somehow, I had to confront my nemesis and defeat him. But how the heck was I supposed to do that?

As we stepped off the elevator onto the sixth floor, toward the Surgical Unit, my phone rang. I prayed it was Tye telling me he'd changed his mind and would pull the books. But, instead, it was Donny, the profile photo of his stupid, grinning face making me seethe. *Frig, Love, not now!*

I'd never heard him so frantic. I couldn't make out a single word he was saying. He sounded like a machine gun constantly jamming and re-firing.

"Donny, just a sec." I raced forward and kissed Mutti on the cheek as the orderly wheeled her through the doors into the surgery ward. The doors swung closed.

Morag corralled me against a wall and nodded at me to continue my call.

"Okay, Donny," I said, trying to focus past my aching heart. "Calm down and just listen to me for a minute. It's literally life or death. *Then* you can talk. The Screw says you have forty-five minutes to pull your videos of me chasing after him or he'll kill us all. That includes *you*, got it? He says you've made five more. How could you humiliate me like that, Donny? I'm supposed to be your friend, man, not some fuzzin' character you cooked up just to make yourself famous. And how in the hell did you even find enough material to make all those videos?" I paused to catch my breath. "Anyway, what's most important is The Screw's freaking out because you outed him. He doesn't want any evidence pointing back to Shadow or to him, and that's *exactly* what you've done—put evidence online, where millions of people will see it! You've put us all in danger."

"None of that matters right now!" he said, gasping for air, coming down from whatever high he was on.

"What do you mean that doesn't matter right now? Pull down those fuzzin' videos *now*, Love, or I'll pound you!" A passing doctor glared at me.

"Sorry," Morag said to him. She turned back to me. "Keep your voice down, babe."

I barely heard her over the sound of email messages, dinging my phone, rapid-fire. I pulled the phone away from my ear to check them out as Donny blethered.

Emails: ninety-nine and counting! One was from Michelle Green, Steven's ultimate fantasy girl back in high school, wondering if I'd seen him lately and did I have his email. And *Hollywood Tonight. You've got to be kidding!* And one was from Audrey Craig, another girl we'd known from Irondale Collegiate, saying she'd always thought I was kinda cute, and she'd love to go on a date so she could run her hands all over my big head, and it got worse from there. Donny was responsible for this! After saving my family, I vowed to kill him.

I slammed the phone back against my ear.

"Spray-painted 'Shut Down the Videos or Die' on our garage door," Donny squawked. "And my parents' garage door, too!"

My stomach dropped. "Oh crap, Donny. Now do you believe me? The Screw's a killer. You have to remove the videos. I think you've got maybe thirty minutes."

Donny's voice got suspiciously quiet. "I can't remove the videos."

There was a buzzing in my head. "Why the fuzz not? How hard can it be?"

"Norb, old buddy, I hope you can forgive me, but the videos are so amazing they can't be removed. I mean, I could, I guess. But should I? Between the five of them, I've got over two million views, easily a hundred thousand likes, a thousand comments, mostly positive, and one-hundred and twenty-two thousand new subscribers. I've got advertisers, paying me to run their ads. Not only am I getting famous, finally, after all these years of trying, and trust me I deserve it, but so are *you,* buddy! This is a once-in-a-lifetime opportunity for both of us. Trust me. I've even tied the Humpty Dumpty YouTube phenomenon in with my *InTown* column. I'm writing about *you,* buddy, and my editor really digs the new angle. Says it's as good, if not better than my *Making Steven Famous* columns. It's re-booted the old readership, and just like the Steven columns, it's selling more papers. Bob Chamberlain couldn't be happier!" He bellowed into the mouthpiece. "The Village Vigilante strikes again!" He laughed at his own joke. "Norb, you should see the tons of fan mail I'm getting from old schoolmates. Fucking amazing, but also a little weird, to be honest. Hey, did you see yourself on the news, being interviewed in front of your shop? Great for business, brother. Now more people know about you and your store. Oh, and you're also on the CHCH news website, under breaking news of course. Even that's going viral. I'm sending you a link right now. And don't forget to check out the new videos, Norb, old buddy. They'll blow your frickin' mind."

The buzzing in my head was so loud that I could barely hear myself holler at him. "I'll blow your frickin' head off, Love, with a twelve-gauge shotgun! You fuzzin' *arse*-hole, Donny!"

I was vibrating with rage. A runner of drool was suspended from my lower lip. Morag's face was tight with disgust and contempt—she'd leaned in and heard the whole conversation. She'd always felt, on some level, that Donny was the worst friend, and now I totally agreed with her.

Donny's words shot out of his mouth. "Look, Norb, I get it! You think I've been totally high-handed with this. But you need to see the bigger picture. To be honest, I was *there* Saturday night. I'd just finished taking photos of my billboard for my website and noticed your Vespa parked in your mom's driveway, so I thought I'd pay the two of you a visit. Your mom was always so nice to me as a kid."

He laughed, crazily. "It was the magic of the universe, really. There I was, walking towards your mom's house and all of a sudden you're flying out of it like fucking Humpty Dumpy high on speed and you're chasing The Screw's bad-ass car like the kick-ass vigilante you were born to be. Shit, Norb, I was so proud of you I could have wept!"

"Well, Donny, when you put it that way." Of course, he didn't notice the acid in my voice. When Donny was high on himself, nothing could penetrate his ego-armour. Arse-hole.

Donny started singing the Ghostbusters theme song, changing the lyrics to "I ain't afraid of no Screw!" He sang it over and over and over like a broken record.

I raised my voice to be heard over his crappy singing. "I bet you're the one who called the news guys to my shop this morning, weren't you?" I looked at Morag and I could tell she was proud of me for standing up to Donny. But before I could utter another word, Donny hung up.

Then things got way worse.

Tony called me, then John. And they were freaking the heck out. The Screw had spray-painted their garage doors, too. And Donny had told Tony that he was going to deal with The Screw in his own way. "Because, what could go wrong with fuckin' Donny bloody Love at the helm?" Tony had shouted into the phone so loud I'd thought he'd deafened me permanently. "*Everything*, that's what! Norb, man, I'm so fuckin' sorry I didn't take you seriously yesterday. Goddammit! What a shit show!"

I'd never felt so fuzzed-up in my entire life, or so scared. Morag was gnawing her lip. I'd never seen her look so worried. What kind of husband was I? I should be protecting my honey. I should be pulling a John McCain, bare feet on broken glass. *Yippee-ki-yay, motherfuzzer!*

"What are we going to do, Norbie?"

"I was going to ask you the same question."

Chapter 10

IT WAS GOING TO BE at least four hours before we would be able to see Mutti, between her surgery and her time in recovery. We'd decided to head home for a bit. Morag had insisted I drop her off at the library so she could dash off her administrative work. Our world might be coming to an end, but orders still had to be filled and work schedules assigned. She said it would only take a few minutes and she'd return home in a jiff so we could figure out our next move. "And eat something babe. A sandwich. And an apple. You know how you get."

Reluctantly, I'd agreed, but I couldn't shake the deep worry that somehow The Screw would be inside waiting to ask her for the best instructional book on how to ensure that Humpty Dumpty had such a great fall that his friends couldn't put him back together again. Plus, I remembered how he'd leered at Morag's breasts. What if he came after her at work?

After I gulped down a torpedo sub, barely tasting it, I was pacing the floor in our apartment living room, plagued with worry over Mutti, my friends, my wife, myself, and our parents. My hands were trembling. I checked my watch. Five minutes until The Screw killed everyone. *Fuzz!*

Then I did what I often did when I was freaking out with worry, other than playing the harmonica, horribly. From the front closet, I shoveled out my old goalie gloves, blocker and stick, went to the full-length mirror on the outside of our bedroom door, and pretended I was making spectacular saves. In my head, I heard the crowd cheering me like they had goalie legend Johnny Bower. Every few saves, I'd run to the window and look for signs of the dwarf on the street below. Then I'd run to the door and press my ear against it, listening for the tippy-tap-tap of The Screws's weirdly long shoes.

Then I shucked my hockey gear and donned my headband.

Determined to be ready to fight him like a real man, I slipped my Hung Gar Kung Fu instructional video into the tape player and busted out my Tiger Crane moves, physically and mentally preparing myself to battle the evil dwarf. In no time, I was gasping like a sweaty, tuckered-out pig. I checked my watch. *Two minutes before we all die.* I busted out twenty push-ups, which wasn't bad for Humpty Dumpty, or whatever the fuzzin' people were now calling me, and the exertion nearly gave me a coronary. But here's the thing about Kung Fu—if you start training the stuff you learned twenty years ago, most of it comes back, and you can get back into killer shape. I'd been practicing hard every day for six months. I felt like a Kung Fu hero, like I was still in my twenties, when I'd earned a brown belt with Master Po at Black Tiger Hung Gar Institute.

I banged out ten inside circle kicks, *almost* throwing out my back. Using the Iron Shirt Chi Gung exercises Master Po had taught us, I slowed my breathing. I would do anything to protect Morag and my family against any and all evil. I'd even protect that knucklehead, Donny. *Fuzz, why was it so hard to hate that guy?*

Now it was no minutes until certain death!

My phone rang and I just about fell over with shock. It was Donny. "This better be good, Donny!" I roared.

"Grab Morag and boot over to the Tartan Club. And make sure you're not being followed. Hurry! Your life depends on it!"

Dial tone.

I rarely trusted Donny. But this time something in his voice had sounded almost sincere, and that was a rarity. Besides, what other options did I have?

I grabbed the sub I'd saved for Morag out of the fridge, whipped outside, jammed the sub in the compartment under the Vespa's seat, and throttled across Steel Street to the library.

I ran through the library doors and hollered, "Morag Reingruber, meet me outside. Hurry!" Then, I raced back outside.

Seconds later, she was out the doors looking pretty darned worried. I hauled her by the arm down the steps to my scooter and handed over her helmet and sub.

There was a look in her eye. I couldn't really blame her. "Morag," I growled. "You need to trust me. Put on your helmet. Get on the Vespa. Eat your sub. I have to save you. Let me be your hero."

Her expression was almost, hopeful?

Off we went. The whole time I kept wondering if it was possible for Humpty Dumpty *not* to be noticed driving a bright orange scooter with a hot redhead riding on his lap, backwards, eating a sub. At least this time I wasn't wearing Morag's tights, I told myself.

I knew we'd be scorching lucky to make it to the Tartan Club without The Screw seeing us and popping our skulls with bullets. Mine, of course, was an easy target. I really did have the biggest head of anyone I'd ever seen.

Chapter 11

TO AVOID DETECTION, I'd veered off busy Steel Street and sped along Burr Street, past the Irondale Community Center, and across Sludge Road. I took a winding bumpy footpath through Bucky Park, then booted along the rail trail, down through dense foliage and into the parking lot behind the Tartan Club.

We came to a skidding stop at the back. Donny had insisted we enter through the rear door.

The only other social club I'd ever been to had been the Germania Club, downtown. It was the German version of the Tartan Club, a little piece of home. Somehow, after all these years, its doors were still open. My parents and all the other German immigrants of their generation had spent decades dancing and socializing there. But once I'd became a teenager, my family stopped going. That was pretty typical, I think. I was pretty sure that nothing was ever the same once your kids became adolescents.

The Tartan Club, as far as I knew, had been sitting dormant for a good twenty years. I guessed that the second-generation Scottish Canadians weren't pining for the old country, either. It was a squat cinder-block building. On the north wall, beside a boarded-up window, there was a Sold sign. At the bottom of a cracked concrete ramp was a large roll bay delivery door. That's where Donny stood, impatiently waving us over.

I drove us inside, and he rolled the door down behind us with a boom, as if sealing us in a tomb. It was creepy.

I turned off the engine. As my eyes adjusted to the dim light, I didn't know whether to laugh, cry, or freak the heck out at what I saw.

Chapter 12

MORAG AND I SLIPPED off the Vespa, yanking off our helmets.

It was like a scene from "This Is Your Life!", or maybe like that moment when all the abductees are reunited aboard the Mothership. There was a little crowd of refugees, and every single one of them looked royally pissed off.

An old man was pointing his finger at me like a pistol, his thumb fully cocked. His Scottish accent was the thickest I'd ever heard it. The man, of course, was Archie Love, Donny's annoying, over-the-top dad. *Oh Gawd, not you, not now.*

"Esme, is *that* the wee egg-heeded boy that used to play wi' oor Donny?" He scoffed, then hissed. He took a slug of McEwan's beer from a can and crinkled his face. "Brutal," he announced, but despite the taste, took another swig. "Ach, that'll do."

He tucked a fag back into his mouth. "Norbert, lad, are you still rotting in your mom's basement?" The cigarette bobbed around as he spoke. A set of rusty keys hung out of his slacks pocket.

I laughed nervously. "Moved out, Mr. Love, a year ago, right after Morag and I married. Run my own comic book store now."

"It's about time," he muttered.

Everyone who was potentially in The Screw's crosshairs was there—Mr. and Mrs. Valentini, Mr. and Mrs. Pappas, Mr. and Mrs. Love, John, Tony and Angela and Angelina, Allison and Stewart, who was now fussing and crying in his mom's arms. They stood glaring at me as if I'd just set their houses on fire, which I hadn't and wouldn't because I'm not a fuzzin' arsonist.

Tony's grown-up kids weren't there. Frankie had gone to work as a truck driver in Calgary, and his two oldest daughters were off at university. I wondered if Tony had warned them about The Screw. How far was The Screw willing to travel to kill family? Also, did second and third cousins count?

We were standing inside a large, musty-smelling kitchen, where steak pie, mashed tatties, neeps, and trifle had been prepared, once upon time, to feed famished young Scottish immigrants after a day working at the steel factory, to fuel them up for a night of drinking and dancing. My parents' generation had done the same at the Germania Club.

On a corner shelf there was a tiny old Toshiba television, the kind with the rabbit ears. The kind you would have been thrilled to have in your bedroom when you were thirteen. Someone had turned it on. The reception was fuzzy but somehow it still worked.

"Dad, where did you get the beer?" Donny asked out of the blue.

"Ach, thirty-eight years ago I stashed a case of McEwan's under that wee stage up front. For emergency purposes. I can stash a beer better than any man I know, right, Esme?"

"Aye, like you stash your common sense, Archie. Up your bumhole."

"You're cruisin' for the bruisin', hen!" he shouted. "Now shut your pie-hole before I shut it for ya." He studied his beer, then looked up at Donny. "Ach, it's a wee bit flat, but beggars can't be choosers." He eyed me, then Donny, and swigged hard, grimacing.

Donny was shaking his head, his lips pursed. His parents really were the Hamilton champs of public arguing. There should be an award for that, I thought.

"*Mannaggia!*" Mr. Valentini cried out, his accent almost as thick. He was gesturing impatiently. "Donny, what is this all about? What are we doing in this God-forsaken place?" He stared at me with fire in his eyes, expecting me to have an answer if Donny didn't.

"God-forsaken place?" Mr. Love said. "This is a bloody shrine. Beats the shite out of the Italian Club. Oh aye, let's stuff our faces with spaghetti and meatballs so the blood drains from our brains, so we can forget how bloody long it took for us to smarten up and join the Allies."

He scoffed again. "Oh, aye, Hitler's bad news, guess we should jump ship."

Then, Mr. Pappas blasted Mr. Valentini. "We will never forget when the Italians invaded from Albania." He laughed darkly, wagging his finger at Mr. Valentini. "And *we* pushed you back into Albania. And, Mr. Love is right, Italy sided with the Nazis before they finally smartened up and joined the Allies. But we Greeks *never* forget."

"Shutta' your mouth, Lamb Chop," Mr. Valentini said. "You Greeks don't know nothing. And, more than that, I don't like the way you're disrespecting to me. Or you, Braveheart want-to-be!"

"Dad," Tony growled, "drop it! We have bigger fish to fry!"

"Agreed," said John, staring daggers at his dad.

Mrs. Love grabbed Mr. Love by the ear and pinched hard, making him squawk. A mean tactic, but it got his attention.

I glared at Donny. "Tell us why we're here, Donny. *Now.*"

"I saw you on the tv this morning. You're too nice to be a vigilante, Norbie," Mrs. Valentini said, placing her hands over her heart. "It will destroy you. Please stop this nonsense."

"Mama's right," said Angela. "Have you lost your mind, Norb?"

"Mama, Angela, forget about that right now," Tony said, "Let Donny speak!"

Donny was trembling, as he always did when he was caught with his hand in the proverbial cookie jar. "This is going to sound crazy, but, as Tony, Norb, and John know, an evil man known as The Screw is threatening to kill all of us and we have to take it very seriously."

"What?" said Mrs. Valentini. She searched everyone's faces to see what they made of this bizarre statement.

Mrs. Pappas scowled at Donny. "You're no good, Donny Love! Johnny has told me and Nico about all the terrible things you've done. Why don't you leave everyone alone, eh? What's wrong with you?"

Donny launched into a completely truthful, thorough, manic-sounding monologue.

Mr. Valentini looked as though Donny had stripped his prized fig tree. Mr. Love was speed-puffing his cigarette, and Mr. Pappas looked ready to clobber Donny over the head.

The women in the room were looking for the nearest exit.

Donny finished with, "The Screw will hunt us down and kill us, but only if he can find us. No way will he think to come here. It's the perfect hiding spot."

"Why haven't you called the police?" Mrs. Pappas said. "My sister's brother-in-law is H.P.D. He's a good man. He'll help catch this Screw."

"The Screw said no police," Donny said.

John added his two cents. "Guys, he's going to try to kill us, so what do we have to lose? Maybe the police *can* help."

"Maybe we should at least file a report," Tony said.

"Look, there's no time for that!" I blurted. "Thanks to Donny, it's zero hour! If he had just taken down those idiotic videos, we'd have more time. But, no, Donny always puts himself first. Anyway, Mutti's having an emergency operation and I have to get back to the hospital. I need to go see her. And if The Screw finds out we called the cops, he'll kill us yesterday, just like he said he would." I wasn't really sure if I was making any sense.

"Is your mom gonna be okay?" John asked.

"I dunno," I said. "I'm going to the hospital to find out, then I'm going to find The Screw and his dirty thugs and cave in their fuzzin' heads with my goalie stick."

They all stared at me. *Maybe now they'll respect me,* I thought absent-mindedly. Obviously, getting a publishing deal wasn't enough to warrant their respect, but potentially bashing in a bad guy's head was.

"I'm coming with you, Norbie," Morag said.

"No," I said. "If I die before Mutti, not that I'm saying she'll die, but, what I mean to say is you'll need to care of Mutti because I'll be dead."

She hesitated. For once, she knew I was right. She grimaced, and threw her arms around me. She whispered into my ear. "Babe, be very careful. And don't rule out calling the cops, okay? Promise me you'll do that, Norbie, if things get really bad. Okay? I need you in my life, big man. So much."

"Oh-my-golly!" Mrs. Pappas broke in.

Everyone followed her stricken gaze. On the tiny television, a Channel 11 reporter was delivering breaking local news. When he spoke, his white Cap'n Crunch moustache billowed under his big nose like soft clouds. Mrs. Pappas had turned up the volume.

It was a clip of me leaving the back door of my apartment as I was on my way to pick up Morag at the library. A female reporter was trying to interview me as I mounted my Vespa. I sounded like a manic Munchkin. What really freaked me out was how fast I was jabbering to the reporter.

"Look, I'm past hammering drumsets and mugging for the camera, and, no, I don't live at home anymore. I live in an apartment with my wife. I'm a small business owner *and* I've published a book. For real! But, *nooooo*, I'm the Village Vigilante, or Humpty Dumpty, or whatever the fuzz the crazies in this town say I am." I gripped my huge head. "Jeepers lady, don't you realize how nuts this sounds? And why is it happening? Because the *biggest* crazy in this town is Donny Love, and he's back on the bullsheet wagon again—that's why! Lying through his fuzzin' teeth! And now everyone else is buying his lies! What the heck is wrong with everybody, anyway?"

Then, as I throttled my Vespa and roared away, I was still ranting.

"Ach, you sound just like oor Donny," said Mrs. Love, dovetailing her hands on her hips. "Bletherin' away about nothing! What a bloody shame. I thought you were better than that, Norbert."

I cringed. I couldn't meet Morag's gaze.

Get out of your head, Norb. You have a ticking bomb to deal with first!

Everyone started firing questions at me, but I ignored them. I pecked Morag on the cheek and ripped out of the Tartan Club on my scooter, its single cylinder firing fast and hard under my weight.

Morag ran out through the bay door and called out, "Call me as soon as you know something! Tell Mutti I love her!"

She turned and hurried back through the roll bay door. It shut behind her, sealing her inside the Tartan Club. I felt like I'd never see her again.

A heavy mix of sadness and fear coursed through me as I throttled towards the rail trail. My mind shifted to The Screw. I prayed he wasn't on his way to kill Mutti. Was he capable of murdering a sick, bed-ridden, defenceless old lady? Was anyone that fuzzin' evil?

Well, obviously.

Yes.

I focussed crazy hard on getting to the hospital as fast as possible.

Chapter 13

I'D ORIGINALLY PLANNED to stick to the streets, but then a powerful rage took over my common sense, and I was really digging the way it made me feel. The mid-afternoon sun beat down on me.

I blasted north down Steel Street in full Vespa glory, praying The Screw would confront me. I wanted to leap off and fight him face-to-face, like a real man, one Morag would totally be proud of, a final and memorable Village-Vigilante-versus-The Screw showdown, traffic stopped, horns blaring, crowds cheering, as I busted out my Kung Fu moves and kicked the little creep's ass.

I wondered if he had the nerve to shoot me in broad daylight. Thinking that kinda killed my revenge fantasy.

Only a coward needs thugs for back-up, Mr. Screwhead. You're nothing but a two-bit fuzzin' chalksucker! This almost-swearing was really growing on me. Morag would be so darn proud of me.

Halfway to the hospital, I suddenly pulled over. Sanity had finally penetrated my thick skull. I could find out how Mutti was doing without putting myself in more danger. I couldn't help anyone if I was dead. Also, Tank and Harlan were sitting ducks, working at the shop, completely unaware that an angry killer dwarf might roll in off the street and obliterate them, just because I'd imagined an Invisiblator.

My first move was to make sure Karl was in the loop. I rolled the Vespa in behind the gas station, out of sight, and pulled out my cell.

I called Karl, steeling myself to explain this insane situation *yet* again, but he cut me off.

"Morag told me, Norbie. Don't you worry about your mother. I've got my nephew here with us. He's a big boy and he works security at the casino in Niagara Falls and has a handgun license. We're not going to let anybody lay a finger on Anna."

I wanted to feel relieved, but I couldn't. "And the surgery? How'd it go? Is Mutti awake?"

Karl paused. "No, not yet. They say that's normal. There was a lot of cancer in there. They got most of it, but they couldn't get all of it. So, your mother's not...cured. Sorry, son."

I felt empty where I knew I should feel panic. So, I cracked a joke.

"Karl, if The Screw shows up, dazzle him with your famous Exploding Tennis Ball trick, then bust his chops."

"You betcha', Norbie," he said, his baritone voice the smoothest I'd ever heard it. He really did sound like Count Dracula, if the Count came from Sarnia, Ontario.

The next step involved going to the shop. It was risky, but I was close, and what I had to say to Tank and Harlan was best done face-to-face.

As I chugged through the intersection, I was relieved to see there were no more media clinging to the shop. I passed the Blue Ball and whipped left into the Tim Horton's parking lot. I weaved through pick-up trucks and locked my scooter to the cedar behind the bowling alley.

The tarring of the roof was in full swing. I loved the smell of hot tar, but today it made me feel queasy. The day's humidity was brutal. Normally, it would slow down a big guy like me, but today I was too fired up. I unlocked the bashed-up delivery door and hastily closed it behind me.

Tank and Harlan were in full debate mode and barely blinked at me. I opened my mouth to speak, but Harlan raised his voice to shut me up. I grit my teeth —I hated when he did that to me.

"*Mercury, Power, Make-up!*" Tank said, quoting *Sailor Moon*. "It's *obviously* a feminist statement. Woman have *power* and they can wield it any way they choose." She stuck a gumball in her mouth. Beside her, a pale kid with green hair carefully examined a Pokemon figurine inside my glass display case. I think he was interested in where this debate was going. He'd also had a crush on Tank for two years.

"Oh, *puh-lease*," Harlan groaned from his usual spot behind the counter. "It's all about the hypersexualization of pre-teen girls. The whole ribbon thing, wrapping her up like she's a sexual gift, the high heels, and, oh, let's not forget the beaucoup lesbian undertones."

"You're such a dick, Harlan. I like you better when we talk about PacMan."

"Okay, I still say PacMan's a *Smartie*."

"*Kuchi*," said Tank. "The Japanese symbol for mouth. Do your research, old man! A *Smartie*? Yeah right! *Pfft*."

"Uh, there are some pretty crazy things going down right now," I interrupted loudly. "Basically, when I was at ComWorld, this evil little hitman who calls himself The Screw delivered a threat from his boss. It seems that the device I invented in *The Steeltown Avenger*—the Invisiblator—well, it's a *real* thing."

I stopped for a sec, waiting for the inevitable "Hey, you're certifiable" or "Ha, Ha, good one", but Tank and Harlan just stared at me, alarmed. So, I continued. "Uh, anyway, The Screw's boss is furious that I lifted the curtain on his nefarious operation, and I was ordered to remove every one of my books from every single store by tomorrow at nine a.m. or The Screw will kill me and everyone I love. Oh, and my idiot friend Donny uploaded the videos of me chasing The Screw's car—"

"Oh, yeah, the Village Vigilante. I meant to tell you. I totally dig those!" Tank interrupted.

Harlan shrugged. "Meh. I would lose the tights. Not very figure-flattering."

Tank looked outraged. "Hey! Fat-shaming!"

"Guys! You're missing the big picture here. The deadline is null and void now. The Screw is coming for me. Right *now!* So I want you both to go home. We're closing up. And we're staying closed until this nightmare is fuzzin' over and everyone is *safe!*"

Behind me, the front window shattered. We all jumped three feet in the air. I may have screeched like a little girl, too.

Outside, there was a swell of voices.

Tank threw her helmet on, growling.

I bolted toward the door, when it swung open and a tall, muscular guy with a brush cut grabbed my wrist and hauled me outside.

"The Village Vigilante!" he cried, "Aryan and proud! Ridding Hamilton of scum, one immigrant at a time!"

One immigrant at a time? What the—?

A harsh roar of approval went up from a crowd of at least fifty Neo-Nazi skinheads. One kid couldn't have been older than eight. They wore white t-shirts, combat boots, black jeans, and waved huge flags. But they weren't alone. A Rainbow Army was marching on the other side of Flux Road, swinging their own placards. They were all singing "We Are Family". I saw several unicorn horns and at least one feather boa. Some had rainbow shields and easily blocked the rocks and garbage that the skinheads were flinging at them.

The next thing I knew, the Rainbow Army was charging across the street, on the offensive, dodging the passing cars. Some drivers pulled over to the curb to watch. Before I knew it, a bunch of neo-Nazis had hoisted me up onto their shoulders and were parading me around as if I had scored the winning goal. I couldn't struggle—they were that strong and efficient.

"Put me down, you guys!" I peeped. "Yes, I'm German. But I'm not a Nazi. I'm just a nerd, OK? I'm a married man, and the only thing I'm really proud of is my wife and my mom. Geez, what the heck!" But my words fell on deaf ears. They'd begun chanting, "*Heil,* Humpty!" at the top of their lungs. It was a nightmare.

Then the skinheads and the Rainbow folks were clashing in the middle of the street. It was *Call of Duty* meets *My Little Pony.* Cars kept honking. Brakes kept screeching. The air was filled with shrieks and roars. There must have been at least a hundred rioters. "Go home,

Nazis," a kid cried from the back seat of his parents' car. "Kill the faggots!" yelled a teenager from his car. His friends were guffawing, and they all began chanting "Kill the fags!" *What the hell? Why is everyone suddenly so evil?*

"Put me down," I yelled, but the skinheads ignored me. I was feeling sick. The ride was getting very bumpy and my upper body kept sinking down lower than my hips. I wanted to vomit all over these goofs. It would serve them right.

The Roofers had ringside seats up above us all. One guy was enjoying a sandwich and a beer, as if he was watching a CFL game.

At some point, Tank had ripped out of the store. In one fluid motion, she launched a flying side-kick at a wiry Nazi's chest, collapsing him to the tarmac. Like a zombie high on speed, he jerked back up into a standing position and lunged at her. They scrapped like wild animals. Harlan slid outside along the front wall, stopped, and began slowly rubbing his fingers against his chin like an arbiter watching a chess match.

"Harlan!" I screeched at him. "Help me!"

He mimed an apology, gesturing to the carnage around me.

As usual, the media flew in like the cavalry, although they definitely weren't. And then, a powerful voice cut through the crap.

"I'll rip out your fuckin' lungs, ya Nazi scum!"

It was Jimmy-the-Barber, daylight glinting off his baldy heed. He was swinging an electric razor by its chord, around and around his head. He flew across the tarmac towards the skinheads. He was still wearing his blue barber's smock and a pair of tattered, old running shoes. A fag dangled out of the corner of his mouth. "Freedom!" he howled, almost choking on the fag as he inhaled.

His razor lasso whacked a guy in the side of the head, buckling him. "Bunch of jumped-up pantry boys, the lot of you!" And he was swinging his razor through a crowd of them, clearing a path. "Die, Nazi scum!"

Reporters and cameraman were spilling out of their vehicles. But where the heck were the police? Just at that moment, my stomach finally heaved, and I vomited all over the two kids holding my shoulders.

The neo-Nazis dropped me like a hot potato. As I fell, I flailed, grabbing at anything I could. Reflexively, I clutched at a sturdy flagpole near me. The fact that a sturdy guy with a swastika armband was holding it helped me to not land on my head. When I realized my terrible mistake, I let go of the flag, but I knew right away I was too late: cameras had flashed, and soon the world would think I was a straight-up Nazi. A neo-Nazi with a barfy beard.

In the distance, the wail of police sirens filled me with hope.

The fascists and the unicorns ran for the hills, taking their injured with them.

Seeing the battle was fizzling out, Jimmy stopped swinging his razor and holstered it in his pants pocket. Although he was out of breath, he'd found the strength to light up another filterless smoke and puff hard. His face was alive with battle.

"Thanks, Jimmy, for having my back."

"Don't mention it, Norbie. Anything for a good neighbour."

"Hey, what about my hair?" shouted a familiar, grating voice. "I haven't got all day."

I couldn't believe my eyes. The Screw was standing in Jimmy's doorway, beside the rotating barber pole, wearing a blue barber cloth. His head was only partially shaved.

He poked his gun against the inside of the cloth. At least I thought it was his gun. His thugs crowded in behind him. My stomach dropped into my Converses. The guy that was going to kill me and my loved ones had been getting an honest-to-God haircut, right beside my shop! *What nerve!*

"He's an ugly bastard, that one," Jimmy whispered. "Makes Frankenstein's monster look like Brad Pitt."

The Screw slowly ran his mitt over the shaved part of his head, eyeing the crowd scornfully. A Channel 11 reporter approached him. He stared past her at the waning battle. "Pathetic!" A passing skinhead dismissively flipped the bird at The Screw. Dwarves were not part of the Master Race.

The Screw laughed it off. "I do my best work *after* a good haircut." Snickering, he turned around to go back inside the barber shop when the reporter reached around and shoved a microphone towards him. When he turned around and she actually *saw* his caved-in face, she backed away in horror.

"I'll be seeing your wife, once I'm done getting pretty for her, Norbie," he smirked at me.

"Screw you, Screw!" I lunged after him, but Jimmy held me back, his anchor tattoo rippling the age spots on his arm. For an old guy, he was remarkably strong.

The Screw and his thugs just laughed at me. "Too many witnesses, Norb," The Screw said, staring past me. "Lucky for you."

"Never mind, lad," Jimmy said, lowering his voice. He muscled me aside. "I wouldnae mess with these men. These bastards *are* killers, trust me on that. So get out of their way, or call the cops if you have to."

He walked back towards his shop, whistling. "Right, Fearless Leader, back inside," he said to The Screw, "and let's put a shine on that baldy heed of yours."

I rushed back into the shop, Tank and Harlan on my heels.

Police were rounding up the stragglers, chasing down skinheads and Rainbow warriors in nearby streets.

"Tape cardboard on the window, Harlan. Tank, lock the door and, no matter what, don't let the media inside!" I noticed Tank's face was scuffed and bloody. *Holy smokes.* But I just didn't have time for her, and I felt bad that I didn't. But I also knew that Tank knew how to look after Tank, and that she'd be okay. I headed upstairs, locking the door to the apartment behind me.

I headed down the back steps to the Vespa, determined to get to the hospital as fast as possible, wondering how on earth I was going to pay for the broken window, and how in the world my silly comic book had turned the world upside down. It was too early for my brain to *really* process the nightmare in front of my shop, so I did what I did best when I was scared out of my mind—I blocked out the bad stuff and just went on autopilot.

Chapter 14

"HOW ARE YOU FEELING, Mutti?"

"I'm fine, Norbie," she said weakly. She squeezed my hand. "I love you, son."

"I love you, too, Mutti."

It pained me to see Mutti so weak and vulnerable. She'd always been such a strong, independent woman. Now, here she was totally dependent on the good will of others, connected to high-tech monitors that blinked alien light. She shared a room in the Critical Care Unit with another woman who was half-watching an episode of *Food 911*, a runner of drool hanging from her chin. She had no visitors. I felt a deep pang for her. If The Screw succeeded in his mission to kill Morag and me, Mutti would be all alone, too. There'd be no one to visit her.

On the other side of the bed, Karl hovered over her. He was weird but he was really starting to grow on me. I wished he had a magic trick that would make cancer disappear. *That* would be a good one.

Dr. Kahn came in, dressed in surgery gown and cap, and stopped at the foot of the bed. "Hi, Anna. How are you feeling?"

My mother smiled at her Doctor. "Well, the pain medication is still working, so I can't complain. And the nurses on shift today are all so good. Very kind. Very hard-working."

That was Mutti for you. Never a complainer.

Dr. Khan gave Mutti's leg a pat. "That's great to hear. I'll be sure to pass that on."

"Dr. Khan," I asked, "how did it go? Will my mother be okay?"

She looked over at Karl.

"This is Karl," I said, "My mother's boyfriend."

Karl looked surprised to hear me call him that. His eyes got teary and he smiled at me. In that moment, I realized just how much he loved Mutti, and that made me want to cry. I didn't want him to lose Mutti, either.

Dr. Kahn met my gaze. "Norbert, as Anna and I have discussed, your mom has stage III ovarian cancer. Although I removed the tumour, I discovered that the cancer has spread extensively to her pelvis. So she will need several rounds of chemo and lots of bed rest at home. This will extend the amount of time that Anna has left."

The amount of time my mother had left?

"How much time is that?" Mutti asked. Her voice trembled a little, which was so hard to hear.

"At the upper end, perhaps five years. But for the majority of patients, it can be considerably less time that."

Mutti met my gaze, but I could barely look at her, I was so upset. She gave my hand a reassuring squeeze.

Karl said, "How can we help Anna, Doctor?"

"Chemo has side effects. The most common ones are fatigue, nausea, and hair loss. Is there someone at home who can take care of her?" The doctor looked to me for an answer, but I was choked up.

"I can," said Karl. He looked over at me. "Norbert, you have to manage the shop, plus that other thing we're dealing with. I don't mind helping out, really. I want to. Anna, is it okay with you if I move in? I can stay in the guest room."

Mutti blinked back grateful tears. "Oh, Karl. That would be lovely. Just lovely. But you stay in my bedroom, with me. No arguments, Norbie. I think God will forgive me this one little sin."

Under other circumstances, it would have grossed me out, but I would have been a giant bumhead to rain on my Mutti's tiny bit of sunshine.

Dr. Khan's face brightened a little. "Good, we'll start chemo in two weeks. Before Anna goes home, she'll receive an information package detailing her treatment, including her first follow-up appointment with me. Any questions?"

Karl shook his head. He was jotting down notes in a little notebook, which was a good thing, because my brain was mush.

Mutti smiled at Dr. Kahn as if she had told her she was going to live forever.

But that was Mutti for you, never one to complain, forever stoic, forever optimistic.

I choked back a sob.

The surgeon reached out, squeezed Mutti's hand, nodded at me and Karl, and headed out of the room.

"Thanks, Doctor," we called after her.

"I'm so sorry, Mutti," I said. I burst into tears and hugged her, making one of the monitors wobble and beep.

"It's okay, Norbie, dear. We all get old and sick at some point. And maybe I'll get five more years."

"Five years isn't long enough. What if you don't get five? What if you only get two? Or one?"

"C'mon Norbie, let's stay strong for your Mutti," Karl said. "Right, Anna?

Mutti nodded.

She weakly patted my arm. "Come on now, Norbie my dear, I need you to be strong. I *know* you're a strong man. Your dad was strong, and I know you are, too." Hearing that my mom believed in me made me want to sob louder. I bit my lip, trying really hard to man up.

"Okay," I said. I took a Kleenex from her bedside table and blew my nose.

"Norman!" Karl cried, suddenly, startled by someone at the door to the room. "What are you doing here? You're supposed to be standing guard!" He looked like he'd swallowed a slug.

A hot-looking guy in a very tight security guard outfit was gyrating in the doorway of my mother's hospital room. He couldn't have been more than nineteen, over six feet of muscle, and he would have been a hit at a ladies' night in any strip club. His soundtrack, coming from his phone, sounded familiar. "Hi, Mrs. Reingruber," he said to Mutti. Then he started singing along, in a really terrible falsetto.

"I like the way you dance, Norman," Mutti said, gently. "Who is this Humpty Dumpty you keep singing about?"

"Stop immediately!" Karl ordered angrily. "This is a hospital, Norman! Not a dance club. I hired you to guard, not dance! Anna just came out of surgery, for God's sake!"

But that sexy freak Norman didn't miss a beat.

"No, it's alright, Karl," Mutti said, raising her head off the pillow, "go ahead, Norman. You're very good." A small laugh escaped her mouth, but the effort was too much and her head dropped back against the pillow.

I was stunned out of my mind. Norman, casino security guard and Karl's nephew, was singing along to Donny's Village Vigilante YouTube video, word for word.

He was dancing like YouTube Humpty, a combination of moon walk, jolted hip hop rhythms, and old school jitterbug, all with big-time stripper vibes. Back and forth he went, jiddering, juddering. He managed to look orgasmic, which was the grossest part.

Then I blew up. I grabbed the phone out of Norman's hand. This was a new video, hot out of Donny's basement studio, showing me dancing up a storm as I faced off against the craziest assortment of spliced-in villains from movie footage. There was the Wolfman, the Thing, Nosferatu, and then, weirdly, Jack Torrance from *The Shining*. Then he'd spliced in today's footage of The Screw, his thugs, Jimmy-the-Barber, and the Rainbow and Nazi Armies battling outside my shop. This particular video was titled, "The Village Vigilante Kicks Nazi Ass!" *Two-hundred thousand hits!* There were dozens of videos on Donny's You Tube channel with links to his Bandcamp account and his *In Town* column. What a selfish, self-promoting bastard!

"Hey, man!" Norman objected. He snatched back his phone. "Hey, do the Humpty, bro', do the Humpty Dumpty." He went back to dancing.

"Enough!" Karl snapped. "Get back outside and keep an eye out for The Screw. That's what I'm paying you to do! This isn't a joke. That man is a murderer, and he's coming after my Anna!"

Norman looked mildly chastened. "Sorry, Uncle Karl. Sorry, Mrs. Reingruber. Just thought I'd see how you're doing and cheer you up a little. I hadn't planned to dance, honest, but it just came out of me. You hear that Humpty Dumpty song in your head and the next thing you know, you're busting out the moves! It's just so catchy. I can barely stop listening to it."

He saw Karl and me glaring at him, and nodded. "Right. Uh, if you or your Mom need anything at all, tell Karl to tell me and I'll get it for you, I promise." Before heading out the door, he turned and looked at me. "Seriously, though, this Humpty Dumpty dance is going to be as big as the Macarena, dude. You'll go down in history." He danced out through the door. It shut behind him.

Donny had single-handedly turned me into a fad, and my Mutti was really, truly dying.

"Norbert, you're going to be okay," Mutti said.

I swallowed a lump in my throat—that was an order.

"Sure, Mutti," I said, forcing a smile on my face. The old woman in the bed next to us had turned up the volume on the Channel 11 News. I thought I was going to vomit—there I was, outside my shop, clutching a Nazi flag, chunks of vomit in my beard. Why was there always a camera around to capture me at my worst moments? I knew *exactly* why.

Donny, you farging icehole!

Chapter 15

HURRYING THROUGH THE hospital parking garage in search of my Vespa, I began to call Morag, but she beat me to it.

"Are you okay?" I blurted.

"I'm fine, Norbie. You're out of breath. What the hell's going on?"

"Mutti has stage III cancer, and it's spread to her pelvis." Somehow I'd managed to force the words past the hot lump in my throat.

She gasped. "Oh, poor Anna. I'm so sorry, babe. Poor Karl."

"Doctor says she might get five years, so that's something, right?"

"Yes, of course, definitely—"

She was cut off by shouts.

"What's going on?" I said, my stomach cinching.

I jumped on the scooter and cranked it to life, zipping south along Mountain Brow Boulevard, phone glued to my ear.

"It's okay, babe. It's the Dads. They're arguing again. This time it's over the dinner menu."

"*That's* what they're arguing over?"

Below, in the lower city, dark clouds pressed against the Hamilton Bay and its ring of steel factories. The stink of industry pricked my nostrils.

"Plus, these doddering old fools all 'know a *guy*' and have ordered in their own artillery. It's like a freakin' munitions depot in here. If this stuff goes off, we'll be blown to kingdom come. Trust me, The Screw's the least of our problems. The sooner you get back here, the better. Hey, I can't hear myself!" she shouted at the Dads. "Shut it for one minute, would ya!" I could tell they'd only half-listened to her. They'd simply lowered their voices as they argued.

"Other than the arguing, are you okay? Do you have food to eat?"

"Are you kidding? I've never eaten so well. Mrs. Pappas is quite the cook."

"Where did she get the food—?"

"Never mind, Norbie, just get us the frig out of here!"

Shouting male voices drowned her out. There was a shriek and the clanging of metal. Morag hung up.

I knew I had to get to the Tartan Club and save the day. *Just add it to the dang list!* Then something made me glance over my shoulder. There was a black car gaining on me.

The Screw's face grinned at me over the steering wheel. *Holy steamroller!* I cranked the throttle of my Vespa. It got louder, but not faster. For the first time ever, it occurred to me that my beautiful orange Vespa was *not* the coolest vehicle on the planet. In fact, maybe it was a *teensy* bit impractical. Maybe a massive, manly Harley would be a better choice for a moment like this. Just as I swung the curve edging Mountain View Park and booted south towards Concession Street, a spray of bullets dinged my gas tank. Startled, I lost control and the bike wobbled. Gas spumed out of the tank, soaking my pants. My heart was jackhammering in my chest. The Screw's bumper was now just inches from my rear wheel.

Sure I was about to croak, I hopped the curb and zigzagged along the park grass, hoping he wouldn't have the nerve to follow me.

Wrong!

The car's engine roared as he shot the curb and raced after me. He skidded around a huge gnarly elm tree, digging up belts of sod. Bullets whizzed past my head. Engine sputtering, I braked hard and leapt off the scooter, flying through the air like a bloated Superman. Somehow I tucked as I landed and somersaulted onto my feet. *Thank you, Sifu Po!* It was too bad there weren't any cameras around to record *that* move for posterity. Next, I did what I knew wouldn't fail. I sprinted the one-hundred-metre dash.

I dashed past two horrified parents, who were grabbing up their kids and hauling them away from certain death, as a black muscle car chased a fat man across their normally peaceful park.

A bullet whizzed past my head. I zigged. I zagged.

I flew across the street and nearly collided with a Canada Post truck. The driver cursed me out and I kept booting. I managed to run between two houses into a back yard but then gassed out hard. I slumped over the chain-link fence, gasping.

I plunked down on the ground like a heavy sack and found myself face-to-face with a yellow Lab puppy. It licked my cheek, glad to have found a new friend. It was really cute. I wondered if Morag and I should get a puppy. For a sec, I went into fantasy land.

Then, on the other side of the house, I heard tires screech. The car doors opened and slammed, and shoes pounded along the driveway.

Other than writing comic books, and rocking the one-hundred-metre dash, there was another thing I was really good at: backyard hopping.

When we were kids, the four of us had driven the neighbourhood crazy, hopping fences, grabbing peaches and plums from neighbours' fruit trees, then leaping into the next yard like maniacal leprechauns. Yeah, it was wrong, but it was fun, and today it might save my life.

After hopping through four yards, I bagged out, predictably. I found myself leaning up against an above-ground pool, gasping for breath. *You're not a kid, anymore.* I listened for a few moments. Except for the dull roar of distant traffic, all was quiet.

I phoned Karl, quietly explained what had just happened, and begged him to order Norman to be extra vigilant protecting Mutti. I made sure I thanked him. I wished I could be the one to protect my mother, but I knew it was Karl's turn now. Mutti had a partner now, a weird one, but a good one, and it was about time. She deserved it.

Now what? Somehow, should I find a way back to the Tartan Club? Nagging doubts paralyzed me. Or should I boot to the shop and try to ambush The Screw? Was I capable of killing him? *How* would I do it, exactly? Half-heartedly, I tried to boost myself up by singing Donny's "I Ain't Afraid of No Screw" song. It didn't work.

My leg was pumping. Waiting for that big lightbulb to flash inside my head, the one that always took forever to go off, I checked phone messages.

My voice mailbox was full! And there were one-hundred and thirty-two emails. I dreaded even reading the subject lines.

All this fuzzin' insanity was a direct result of Donny's selfish ambition. As far as I was concerned, he was The Village Lunatic, and the World Grand Champion Attention-Seeking-Bumhead.

Tye Novak definitely ran a close second, posing as a philanthropic publisher trying to help new authors, which he clearly wasn't. He was only hell-bent on helping himself!

Donny and Tye probably shared the same DNA. *Jerks!*

I scrolled through the list of emails, looking for anything from Morag or the hospital.

There was a voice mail from the Village Lunatic. I listened to it, against my better judgement. Apparently, Donny had a fool-proof plan to foil The Screw. He said everyone was now officially safe at the Tartan Club. They'd even sand-bagged it, and had several working machine guns, ready to blast! This was some kind of bad dream. It was hugely important for me to meet the "buds" at 229 Kingslea Drive, ASAP. "'Use the back door, bro," he'd said, "and approach from the house behind. Think old school backyard-hopping. You can do it, Norbster. I've got faith in you, big guy!"

So, Tony and John had agreed to this crazy plan? In my frazzled brain, I imagined Donny pressing guns to their heads, as he explained his brilliant scheme to them. If it wasn't for the remote possibility that Tony and John might actually go to 229 Kingslea Drive, I wouldn't have considered going.

But my desperation knew no bounds. Why the fuzz had the universe chosen me to be its stupid hero? *Just because I write about superheroes doesn't mean I _am_ one!*

I sorely missed my Vespa. Harley or not, it would have gotten me to Kingslea Drive so much faster. I scrambled to my feet and hopped through backyards, determined to stay undercover. Dogs barked at me. Occasionally, I interrupted a BBQ. My stomach rumbled. And somewhere, I swear, Donny was secretly filming me for his next fuzzin' video.

Chapter 16

FOR MORAG'S SAKE, AS you know, I'd been trying really hard to not swear, but when Donny started explaining his plan this is exactly what shot out of my mouth.

"What the fuck are you on about, Love!"

I was so exhausted from backyard hopping and stopping and starting one-hundred-metre sprints. My Zeppelin t-shirt was soaked. I probably stank. I was wheezing so hard I sounded like the whistling of a boiling tea kettle.

There was a sharp twinge in my chest and I panicked for a sec, wondering if I was having a heart attack. Turned out it was only a cramp from all that running.

"You're the Village Lunatic, Donny, you know that, right?" I clenched my fists. "You're fucking crazier than crazy. And for some really fucked-up reason, you keep wearing that stupid *Making Steven Famous* hat. Why? No one cares! Steven's gone. He grew up. He's not coming back. He's not famous, and neither are you!"

My voice cracked like it always did when I got angry. John and Tony were staring at me in shock. It felt good to see them staring at me with something other than smugness or annoyance.

I decided not to apologize for swearing, or for losing my temper. Honestly, I didn't even feel bad about any of it. I was feeling powerful, for a change, and I was in desperate need of that. And frankly, maybe it was time for my friends to take me seriously.

Through the front window, across the street, I could see Huntington Park Elementary School. It was so ironic. The thing was, I didn't want to be stuck in Grade Five anymore. I wanted to be a man, once and for all.

"One second," I ordered the three of them. I speed-dialed Morag. "Everything okay? Is The Screw there?"

"No, Norbie, no Screw. Everyone's getting along for now. Listen, I want to come help you. I don't want you to go this alone."

"Morag, no. It's not safe outside the Club. Plus, I'm not alone, I'm with the guys, and we have an awesome plan. We're going to end this sheet-show." I looked skeptically at Donny. "Right, Donny?" I mouthed.

"So, what's this awesome plan? Please tell me *Donny* didn't come up with it."

The buds stared at me impatiently.

"Morag, you'll just have to trust me. Besides, I'm not doing this alone, OK? We're a team, the guys and me."

Morag was dangerously quiet for a moment. "Well. You can tell me all about it when you come back. Alive, understood?"

I thought Donny was about to have an aneurysm. His plan was boiling over inside him, and he was pacing like a caged animal.

I hung up, determined to get on with things.

Due to my lifelong habit of procrastination, Morag had taken on most of the major responsibilities in our life, like personal finances, and book-keeping for the comic book shop, and staying on top of our suppliers.

And I suspected, at that moment, surrounded by my old buddies, that my tendency to avoid stuff had not only mentally exhausted Morag, it had eroded her respect for me. I worried that one day she'd leave me, like the time Allison had left Donny. I couldn't handle a life without Morag. I'd rather set myself on fire.

Somehow, I had to regain her respect.

I decided I would hear out Donny's plan, which would no doubt be the worst, most screwed-up plan ever, then come up with a *real* plan to save everybody.

"Okay, so what are we doing here?" I said. "What's this plan of yours, Donny? Let's hear it." Tony and John were looking grim.

We'd all been on the receiving end of Donny's hare-brained schemes, especially in the past year, but somehow, today, at their wits' end, they'd found it in themselves to listen to the Village Lunatic unload his latest bullcrap ploy.

"Start from the beginning," I said. "And go slow. I can barely focus."

Tony nodded his head with profound weariness.

"Okay," Donny said, getting up in my grill to pitch his idea. He was so lit up I thought he would combust. "We disguise ourselves and lure The Screw to your shop, and I piss him off so he draws his gun on me. We keep him distracted so he doesn't actually shoot me. But by then, I've already called the cops, and when they show up, I've filmed the whole thing, and presto, proof's in the pudding, so jail time for the *Screwmeister* and his dirtbag thugs!" He looked at our faces and lost some of his confidence. "Or something along those lines. Hey, at least it's a start, right?"

"Disguises? I said. "Like your silly Saturday morning meet-up group? And he doesn't shoot you because he's so *distracted*? Like an episode of *Batman and Robin* or something? Wow. And people thought *I* was delusional."

Donny eyed each of us. "Come on guys, this could work! Just because it sounds crazy doesn't mean it'll never succeed."

"Okay," I said, hesitantly. "So how exactly would we set this trap?" I couldn't believe I wanted to hear more. I really was that desperate.

Tony's face was a careful blank, but John shrugged.

"I don't know, okay, not really. Like I said, it's a start. I thought you guys might have some ideas to add. Plus, as we're getting into character, we can riff. I do that at the mall all the time, and trust me, mostly it works."

"What?" I said. "So, the full extent of your plan is what you just told us? *That's* it? If you want to run around in a costume, that's *your* business. But don't tell yourself it's going to save the day!"

I looked at solid, level-headed Tony, hoping he'd offer up a better plan, a detailed plan, but he just threw up his hands. "I mean, as fucked up as it sounds, it almost makes sense. Shit. I don't know anymore." He sighed. He looked at John, then shrugged. "It's not like we have a long list of alternatives."

John just studied his shiny shoe, completely avoiding the issue.

"What's the real reason for the disguises, Donny?" I said. "So you can secretly film us? And at the end of it all, we'll all be dead. But hey, at least there were millions of views, right?"

A snort of laughter from John reminded me how bitter I'd become. If I weren't careful, I'd end up just like him. But I was still steaming mad.

"You got it wrong, Norb," Donny said, raising his index finger to make a point. "This is about defeating The Screw, not about me making videos. And I've got my own crack team, *and* they're willing to work for free. They owe me more than a few favours."

"Someone owes *you* a few favours?" I said. "Well, that's a switch. So where the hell are they? Locked up in the attic? And *whose* fuzzin' house is this, anyway?"

Donny ran through the kitchen and whipped opened the basement door. I wondered if he was about to summon up Hannibal Lecter from the bowels of the house.

"Patricia," he called, "are you ready for us?"

"Ready when you are, darling."

That wasn't creepy. Nope. Not at all.

He turned his back to us, all lit up. "Patricia's our Incognito Club Master. Every Saturday morning, me and my Incognito friends meet up and her team disguises us, so we can go to the mall and pretend to be anyone we want to be, famous people, too. Sometimes she even joins us." Donny had apparently snorted six bags of cocaine—his eyeballs were literally trying to pop out of their sockets.

"You guys have to try Incognito! It's totally dope, man!"

"Totally *dope*," John said, finally, "yeah, right."

"Sure, Donny," I said, "I'll get right on that!" Sometimes, I found it endearing when he tried to hard sell you an idea, bizarre or otherwise. But not on that day. He'd sounded like he was pressuring us to join a BDSM club, not a dress-up party.

Now, as if he'd exorcised his demon, a calm came over him. He motioned us to follow him down into the basement. And for some stupid reason, we actually did. We were *that* desperate.

At the bottom of the stairs, I heard Burt Bacharach's song, "Say A Little Prayer", playing through a stereo speaker. I followed the music into the rec room.

The basement was practically a Hollywood make-up trailer. Costume racks lined the walls. Four dressing-room mirrors, topped with bright light bulbs, hung on the old, wood-panelled walls. In front of each mirror, there was a white leather barber chair. This was not your typical Village bungalow basement, far from it. The make-up artists were gawping at me, star-struck. I really didn't like the feeling of being a celebrity. It wasn't the awesome feeling I'd expected. In the past few days, I'd realized just how much I *didn't* like people staring at me.

A beautiful black woman with the biggest Afro I have ever seen came up to greet us. "Hello, I'm Patricia," she said, shaking our hands. She was very tall and wore lots of big, chunky rings on her fingers, and a sixties-style pantsuit, and platform shoes. "Let's meet the rest of my crew before we get started, shall we?" She beckoned to a big guy on our left.

"You're the Humpty Dumpty guy," he said like it was a compliment or something. He winged out from behind his chair and busted out the Humpty Dumpty dance. He was really good at it, but I could barely keep a polite smile on my face. Would people *ever* forget about Donny's stupid videos?

His right hand was missing two fingers. He was almost as heavy as me, but very tall. I'm six-feet-two, and he towered over me. His black hair was short, his dark eyes piercing. He was wearing red leggings! He caught me looking at them and smiled shyly. "Red leggings are in," he purred, "thanks to you." He extended his hand. "I'm Darryl. Glad to be rockin' your world, Humpty."

It was official— everyone in the fuzzin' world had lost their mind!

A skinny guy in a New York Dolls t-shirt was giving me the once-over. "Sir Humpty Dumpty, cleaning up the Hammer, one dirt bag at a time!" His hair was pure Flock of Seagulls. A safety pin stuck out of his cheek. I tried not to stare, especially since it made me feel queasy.

"You, sir, can call me Dead Man," he said graciously. "And I want you to know how honoured I am to be in your presence."

I just wished everyone would stop treating me like I was royalty. Out of the corner of my eye, I could see John smirking at me. *Fuzz you, John!*

"Cool," Patricia said. She clapped her hands. "Introductions are over, let's get to work." She flashed me a lovely smile, full of pearly teeth. "Donny has filled me in on your situation, so I know exactly how to make this work." I was glad she was confident, because I sure wasn't. The whole plan was cockamamie.

Each make-up artist had grabbed one of us and led him to a chair. Tony looked worried, but John looked kinda thrilled, like the time Mrs. Sawchuk chose him to help her demonstrate the jitterbug in our Grade Six Fun Day workshop.

"So, who do you want to be, Norbie?" Patricia asked

I was confused. "Who? Uh, sorry, I thought you guys were just gonna make us look unrecognizable. I didn't realize you were going to disguise us as actual other people." What the heck? This wasn't ComWorld, for fuzz sake.

John was looking at Patricia and me in his mirror's reflection. "Make him into John Candy, a very German John Candy, complete with Lederhosen and an Oktoberfest hat." He was grinning like a Cheshire Cat. *Fuzzin' Fuzz you, John!*

"Cut it out, Pappas," Tony warned.

"What? What's wrong with John Candy? The guy was funny as hell in *Planes Trains and Automobiles*," John said.

Tony raised his voice, in total dad-mode. "And for once, John, lay off with pushing Norb's buttons. Let's all be cool and let these people do whatever it is they do, so we can figure out our next move." He crinkled his face in the mirror. Tony wasn't looking forward to dress-up time.

That made me feel bad. "Look, Tony," I said, "you guys don't need to dress up. I'm pretty sure The Screw has no clue what you guys look like."

Tony shifted in his chair and pointed a finger at me. "Norb, these days everyone's pictures are splattered all over the friggin' internet. Somehow my high school yearbook picture ended up online, and so did my wedding photo, and I have no idea who put them there or how to get them off. And, trust me, if I ever find out who posted those pictures I'll fit them with cement boots and give them a free swim in the bay. Plus, the guy found our homes and spray-painted our garage doors." He shrugged. "So yeah, I'm sure The Screw knows what we friggin' look like."

For a split second, I remembered Tony at seventeen, his long black hair down his back, a smoke bobbling on his lower lip and a beer in his hand. He'd looked like a hooligan, but he was as sensible and solid as anybody's dad. I shook away the memory. I didn't have time for the past, not the way Donny always did.

"Tone's right," John said. "My photo's on the front page of my business website. Anyone can find me. Hardly anything is private these days. Guaranteed The Screw knows exactly what we look like."

Donny was nodding. "True' dat, Johnny-boy." He seemed completely delighted with the situation.

When this was over, *if* we were alive, I was going to stage a fuzzin' intervention for Donny.

"Fine," I said to Patricia, grimacing. "Candy it is. And what about you, Tony?" My leg was back to pumping involuntarily. I wondered how many calories I was burning.

"Indy driver, of course. And if my psychic abilities are in good working order, John is going to be Mr. Dance Fever himself, John Travolta."

John high-fived Tony. "Ah, you know me well!"

I wasn't surprised at their choices. I knew my friends pretty well, too. "Donny, who are you going to be?"

I wanted Donny to say it out loud, so that maybe for once in his life he'd hear how ridiculous he sounded.

"Steven, of course."

I was barely able to contain myself. "Uh huh. Of course. And what Steven incarnation is it this time? Coen Brothers inspirer? War hero? Rock and roll star saving the world? Huh? Huh?"

He shot me the devil horns and straightened in his chair, grinning cheerfully. I had my answer. He was totally at home in that chair and *that* scared the hell out of me. When Donny was at home with anything, that usually meant horrible news for everyone and anyone connected to him. No wonder most of the people he'd grown up with had ditched him. *You're too fuzzin' much, Love!*

Patricia winked at me, spun me around to face the mirror, and went to work. She seemed very capable. "How will dressing up like John Candy with lederhosen trick The Screw?" I muttered. "The poor guy's dead, this is so disrespectful. What if his family sees me?" I thought about all that for a second. I was pretty sure his family didn't live in the Hammer. Then I realized that dressing up as John Candy was so bizarre that The Screw wouldn't expect it. This plan was all about shock value. Startling The Screw, so he'd forget to pull the trigger for awhile.

Aw, who were we kidding? This was a half-baked, looney scheme, cooked up by a man who was probably certifiable.

Where are you, Steven? I'd bet you'd know what to do. Dang, I thought, *now I'm trying to extract wisdom from a ghost—exactly what Donny does on a fuzzin' daily basis.* After this mess ended, I promised myself I'd stop hanging out with Donny for a full year, and give myself a real chance to grow up.

Well, it turns out Patricia was a genius with wigs and prosthetics. In no time at all, she had me looking exactly like John Candy. I remembered how his voice had sounded as Yosh Schmenge. "Let's dance!" I said to the mirror. I wished I had an accordion.

Truthfully, now I was glad to be here. It gave me time to figure out the next stage of the plan, the part at my shop. Surely planning was way different than procrastinating. It felt pretty different, anyway—it felt responsible. I guessed I really was starting to grow up.

I constantly kept trying to re-assure myself that Donny's half-baked scheme was better than no scheme at all. But not matter how hard I tried I couldn't figure out the second half. My best comic book ideas came out of nowhere. And, of course, writing a great story about dangerous criminals was way easier than fighting them in real life, and that was really saying something, because writing a great story is really, really hard.

I definitely wasn't cut out for fighting real-world criminals. Red leggings or not, I was no hero. I was just a regular guy, and often a cowardly one.

I was jarred out of my obsessive thoughts by the sound of a decisive *snip.*

"What the fuck?" *Sorry for swearing, Morag!*

Patricia had cut off my beard.

Chapter 17

AT SEVEN-THIRTY P.M., we four were walking along Flux Road, headed for the shop. I was still shaky. After Patricia had obliterated my beard, there'd been a few minutes of hyperventilation. The guys had managed to pull me together, but I was feeling like Samson, after Delilah cut off his hair. There was lots I didn't remember from my Sunday school days, but I always remembered Samson, because he was basically a superhero. Well, until someone cut off his beard, that is.

The Lover Boy song "Working for the Weekend" vibrated the windows of the Blue Ball bar as we rolled past. Up beside our apartment window, the Irondale Bowling sign pulsed bloody light against the strip mall's brown brick. Across the street, a customer swung open the door of Mike's Submarine Shop. On the corner, beside the convenience store, the gas station was in full swing. All four corners of the intersection were busy, yet, strangely, despite all the activity, no one had noticed us.

John had practically *danced* his way here. He had a young man's physique. In his white three-piece suit and black shirt, thick black chest hair on full display, and making all the right moves, he looked exactly like John Travolta. All in all, the artists had done an excellent job. Tony wore an actual Sparco racing suit, red and white, and I had never seen him so happy. If Patricia was thinking that she would be getting it back from him when this was over, she had another thing coming. Even I looked amazing in my brown Lederhosen, and green Oktoberfest hat with its cool brown feather. My white shirt was crisp, and I loved my brown suspenders. Mutti would have wanted a framed photo for the fireplace mantel. John Candy surely would have approved. I wondered if Yosh Schmenge would be a legit cosplay role for ComWorld next year. *Well, if I'm alive.*

Then there was Donny. As Steven. As Steven in his Clint Eastwood phase—poncho, bashed-up boots, hat—you get the idea. He even had a cigarillo in his mouth. Together, we four looked like some poor writer at Marvel had gone off his meds.

We arrived at the shop. Donny flew inside like a deranged jackrabbit, adrenalized on danger. Suddenly, John had two left feet. He was terrified to go through the doorway. I grabbed his arm and hauled him inside. I was past feeling shaky, now. It was time to man-up. Tony looked angry, which was really just Tony feeling scared. I'd known him long enough to realize that about him. He flicked on the light and scanned every nook and cranny for The Screw.

Donny had already set up the two webcams, tucked in behind books, already to film from different angles around the shop.

"Okay, last-minute check," I said. "Video on, Donny?"

"Check."

"Media alerted, John?"

"Check."

"Tony, 911?"

"Paid the kid across the street ten bucks to place the call when I give the signal."

"Okay, lock the door, Tony," I said. "Here we go."

My buds eyed me tentatively as I dialed The Screw's number. My phone was shaking in my hands. This had been the plan, but that didn't mean any of us actually *liked* it.

I was so scared I could barely breath.

"I wondered when you'd call." I could hear a smile in his deep voice. A creepy, scary smile.

"Uh, um," I stammered, panicking. I hung up.

Tony looked like I'd pulled out my penis and peed on his white racing shoes, and John looked as if I'd scratched his autographed Saturday Night Fever LP, and Donny-as-Steven Dundee, well, he simply looked disappointed.

"I know, I know, I'm procrastinating. Just give me a minute and I'll try again."

Tony walked over and leaned against the counter, boiling with rage. "Dial the fucking number, Norb, and let's get this over with! We want that asshole here, now. He needs to think he can run over here and kill you. Call him now. Or I'll kill you myself!"

I was about to re-dial when we heard a horrible screeching of tires outside. My insides iced up.

The expressions on everyone's faces told me they were all thinking the same thing. No reason to re-dial The Screw. He'd arrived! *Fuzz!*

Tony took a deep breath, unlocked the front door and then pretended to browse. John and Donny followed suit. They were actually following my plan. Astonishing!

I remembered The Screw's warning: *no cops.*

"Remember guys, improv," I whispered, my voice all cracked and splintery. "Remember the first rule of improvisation, *Say 'yes'.* Second rule, *Say 'yes and'.* Rule number three, *make statements.* Rule four, *There are no mistakes.* I'll start." On game nights, Donny sometimes made me do improv with him, and sometimes, because she had a soft spot for Donny, Morag would join in. Donny was a natural born bullshitter—way better than Morag and me.

I made sure my special music selection was playing *just* loud enough over the shop stereo. Harlan and Tank would have flipped out. Polka music filled Steel Town Comics.

The Screw and his three thugs tumbled inside. Right away, their eyes widened.

"*Guten Abend*, gentleman, welcome to the First Release Club," I said, my accent thick like John Candy as Yosh Schmenge. "Join now and immediately enjoy all the benefits of our VIP club membership, including first dibs on all new monthly releases. Oh, look, the latest issue of *New Avengers* has just arrived, and it's a dandy." I lifted it off the counter and waved it in the air. "As a club member, you can peruse it *almost* privately and decide if you want to buy before the doors open to the public." I guffawed some more and shook my head sheepishly.

"Comic book nerds really are the most interesting people, right, *meine Herren?*" I laughed despite their sullen, angry expressions. "If you join now, you'll not only meet interesting people like yourselves, you'll also receive a hefty fifty percent off the sticker price." I added a tasty yodel, just to highlight the special offer. Good job!

My heart was hammering in my throat. My palms were cold and clammy. They obviously couldn't have cared less about my bogus club membership offer. Their faces were now heavily stitched with anger.

One of the thugs locked the door.

"Where the fuck is Norbie!" The Screw yelled, smashing his huge fist against the counter, upending a Wonder Woman figurine. "And who the hell do you think you are, weirdo? That fat fuck, John fucking Candy?"

He *actually* knew who John Candy was. He didn't seem like a guy who'd watch SCTV, though. Yosh Schmenge was a fairly obscure character, unless you were a Candy fan.

"*Yes,*" John, said, turning around from his phony book browsing, "though the real John Candy is dead, of course, God rest his soul. And no doubt you realized that I am John Travolta from Saturday Night Fever."

The Screw curled his lip at John. My heart sank. Just then, a really lively version of The Chicken Dance started playing, loudly.

"*Ja!* Let's dance!" I inexplicably yelled at John. Suddenly, there we were, Yosh Schmenge and John Travolta, chicken-dancing to save our souls. Donny excitedly joined us. From the look on his face, he'd forgotten that we were about to die. For him, this was just another fun night.

The improv dancing bought us about twenty seconds. Then The Screw shut us down, roughly. His goons had us by the arms, hard, so we stopped.

The dwarf eyed me suspiciously. "Where. Is. Norbert. Reingruber?"

I checked my watch, trying to chuckle just like John Candy. "It's Norbie's turn to buy coffee and donuts. He'll be back in five." I chuckled and threw my hands up in the air. "He's fast on his feet, that Norb. Not bad for a guy as big as Humpty Dumpty." I chuckled some more. "Don't worry, sir, the Egg Man won't be long." I leaned against the counter, shaking my head, forcing a smile past my make-up. "Norbie, now he can polka."

Tony turned around. He'd been pretending to examine action figurines in my rotating display case. He gulped subtly, and lowered his voice considerably. "I'm Mario Andretti. You've probably heard of me. Greatest race car driver of all time? Want an autograph?" He stood in front of the window and gave a long, dramatic stretch. *The signal*, I thought.

One of the thugs brightened. "I love Formula One," he said thickly.

The Screw gave the big guy a dirty look. He shut his mouth and reset his face back to concrete death.

With his good eye, the dwarf scanned Tony suspiciously. His other eye moved by itself and stared right at me. It gave me the willies.

I worked really hard to keep Yosh Schmenge smiling.

"I'm Steven Dundee," Donny blurted, apparently in need of attention. He did a jig, gripping a Superman comic like the deed to a gold mine. I thought his eyes would literally explode out of his skull. "And we are...Incognito!"

"Steven Dundee?" The Screw sneered. "Isn't he that pathetic *do-gooder* trying to save the world? Fighting crime and all that bullshit?" He snorted. "That guy makes me wanna puke." He flicked the air with his meaty fingers. "Why would you dress up like *that* guy?" He eyed us quickly. "And what is this 'Incognito', really, some kind of fucking murder mystery game?"

"Yes," John said, "*and* which one of us is the criminal, do you think? I bet you guys have played this game before." He chortled. "Go ahead, take a guess." John's sarcasm made him sound dangerously courageous.

All at once, The Screw blew a fuse. He jumped up and grabbed John's neck, knocking him against a rack and upending it. His thugs whipped out their guns. John stood up straight, yanking The Screw upward with him. His feet dangled in mid-air. The look on the ugly little creep's face was priceless. John's face got red from the choking he was getting. *What a fuzzin' professional!*

"No one talks sarcastic to me, Travolta," The Screw growled. "No one. Get it!" It was obvious he was struggling to maintain his aura of invincibility. Hard to do while you dangle like someone's necklace.

"Call Norbie now!" the Screw roared. "And tell him to be here in two minutes. Or Johnny Travolta gets it." He let go of John's neck and dropped to the floor. He fished a massive gun out of his belt and pointed it at John's face. Of course, his gun was bigger than anyone else's. That guy definitely had little dog issues. In typical fashion, John smiled sardonically. Behind him, I noticed Tony discreetly sidle over to the door, unlocking it, on cue.

"Hold on," said The Screw, turning from John and staring at me. An evil light burned inside his googly eye. "Your get-up is pretty good, John Candy, or is it Humpty Dumpty? Or the Village Vigilante? It's all pretty impressive, but unfortunately, no matter who or what you try to become, your pathetic Norbieness will *always* shine through!" He triumphantly glanced at the others. "Donny Love, John Pappas, and Tony Valentini!" He scoffed. "I'm way smarter than all you clowns put together. And I know more about all of you than you know about your pathetic selves, thanks to fucking Google."

A shudder wracked my body. But all our ridiculous stalling had paid off.

The door flew open. The media had arrived! I thanked for the invention of police scanners. Channel 11, CHCH TV, Global News, City-TV, they were all here! Cameras were rolling. The Screw hastily shoved his gun inside the back of his belt. John Travolta kept on smiling.

I beamed at the cameras and reporters. "Hi, everybody, I'm Norbert Reingruber, and this criminal is The Screw and these are his evil thugs. Thug One, Thug Two, and Thug Three. And they have guns. They are real-life, cold-blooded killers. And for some crazy reason, they came to my shop to murder us."

A few of the reporters gasped at my revelation. This was going to be some exciting footage, yessir.

I chuckled some more, shaking my head good-naturedly just like Yosh Schmenge. "No idea why they'd want to kill us. Maybe they just don't like comic books, or men wearing Lederhosen."

A hardened reporter asked, "Why are you dressed up like John Candy? What's the relevance?"

"*Well,*" Donny broke in, "we're playing a murder mystery game, and Norb dressed up like John Candy. And that's exactly what you do when you play a murder mystery game. Dress up. Like anyone. It doesn't matter who." He grinned at The Screw. "The Screw loves games, don't you, Mr. Screw?"

The Screw was turning redder by the minute. His hands clenched and unclenched.

Donny pointed his finger at the him. "What's your idea of a *fun* game, Mr. Screw? Get a gun and a blow away a bunch of harmless nerds trying to have a little fun in a nice little comic book shop on a Monday night?"

Tony was shaking his head at Donny, sawing his knife hand across his own neck, trying to get Donny to shut up before he got us killed.

"Hey," asked a hip and very clueless young reporter, "aren't you Danny Devito, the actor?" He gasped at The Screw's googly eye. "Oh my God, Mr. Devito, what happened to your eye?"

"Are you the person seen on YouTube videos recently, who has been called 'The Screw'?" a CBC reporter asked, trying to not to vomit at the sight of his grim eye. "Would you explain your business, sir? How do you respond to these allegations that you are a murderer?"

The Screw shot me a death stare that actually hurt my face.

Then he mumbled something nasty and blew out a big breath. The stink of greasy fried onions wafted over his gold-plated teeth.

He tipped down the brim of his hat, spun smoothly like a bowling ball on a hardwood lane, and, with thugs in tow, broke through the throng of reporters. He growled at their questions and shoved them out of his way.

I'd gambled that he wouldn't be stupid enough to murder us with so many witnesses present. It seemed the gamble had paid off. But we weren't out of the woods, yet.

Police sirens wailed, closer and closer. Relief swept through me. The kid at the sub shop had seen Tony's stretch.

Outside, lit up by the pulse of the bowling alley sign, I could see crowds gathering. Not again! At this hour?

My legs went all rubbery. I couldn't relax until he was behind bars. What would The Screw do to us if the police *didn't* arrest him? If they didn't catch him?

Of course, we'd made things worse—we'd blown his cover. He was as famous as me now. Except he was *infamous*. And furious. Could we have done a worse thing?

The gaggle of reporters and their cameramen had raced after him, but keeping their distance. One had stayed behind. I'm pretty sure he was the same guy who'd interviewed me last year concerning my relationship with my hero Steven Dundee. He looked eager to talk to me.

"Let's do the interview outside," I said, giving him a big smile.

As he'd walked through the door, I locked it behind him and breathed a heavy sigh of relief. It was mean, but there was no way I was going to be interviewed. I couldn't handle any more attention. He glared at me for a moment, then joined the rest of the news people.

The four of us stood at the window and stared at the circus out front. In the flickering red and blue police lights, it was chaos. As The

Screw ripped his creepy black car out over the curb with a terrible screeching of tires, more of the weirdos from the brawl were returning to watch. An orange VW van slid up to the curb, dope smoke pouring out of it windows. Four white kids with dreadlocks slid open the van door and stumbled out, chanting "No more police brutality!" between bouts of hysterical laughter. One of them kept looking back longingly at the sub shop.

The neo-Nazis were back to chanting, "Heil, Humpty!" Man, I was sick of it. *Look at me, man! Does John Candy look like a Nazi to you! Really?* Then I remembered I was wearing Lederhosen.

Police cars lined the narrow strip in front of my shop. At least six officers were starting to do crowd control. Two police cars had U-turned and were tearing down the road after The Screw. I tried not to think about the possibility that they wouldn't catch him.

"Shit," Donny said, "why do all these people show up at almost the same time? It's like everyone owns a police scanner."

"Only in Hamilton," Tony said, shaking his head. "Same shit, different fucking pile. What else is fucking new."

"This Nazi shit has got to go," John said quietly. "Do you have something less German-looking to change into, Norb?" He looked pointedly at my Lederhosen.

"Good point, John. I'll get on that right away. But on a positive note, guys, awesome improv! I can't believe we pulled it off. Thank you so, so much!"

And that's when my phone rang.

Chapter 18

OF *course* we let the police into the shop. But when they got a good look at the four of us, they kept their hands on their firearms for a few minutes, which was a bit insulting. We explained everything, which they had a very hard time believing. Again, a bit insulting. They kept asking me a lot of questions about being a Nazi—*very* insulting. But we gave them the video footage from the cameras, and their interviews with Mutti and Karl and Morag and everyone else at the Tartan Club were going to confirm what we'd told them, so they'd have to believe us, sooner or later. I had a moment of panic when I realized that the police were sending officers over to The Tartan Club, where our crazy families had stockpiled *weapons*, but a subtle head shake from Tony told me he had already looked after it. I advised them to call the Minister of Defence regarding the Invisiblator, but that one didn't even merit a response. Well, when the world order was obliterated, no one could say I didn't warn them.

I emphasized *again* to the officer interviewing me how I was really worried about Mutti's safety, and she said they'd send one of their best to the hospital to keep an eye on her.

Afterwards, I told the guys I needed to be alone.

Tony and Donny and John slipped outside where the police were dealing with some stubborn struggles between the Rainbow and Nazi armies. Donny ran back to Incognito House to get his car. Then he'd pick up John and Tony and take them to their cars.

Truthfully, I would have gone with them, but Morag had phoned and insisted I meet her in the back corner of the parking lot behind the bowling alley. She'd given me zero choice. I wanted her to sit tight at the Tartan Club, and I knew the police would be wanting to interview her, but Morag was a strong woman, and this time she'd really made up her mind. Besides, with the police hot on The Screw's tail, he'd be too busy to track Morag's exodus from the Club. Was she taking a taxi? Or bussing it? Or running here? Like Donny, she was in excellent shape. I wouldn't put it past her.

In the back parking lot, waiting for Morag, I prepared for battle, drilling my old Kung Fu moves. I'd changed out of my Lederhosen and into my old *gi*. It was perfect for battle. Plus, now no one would mistake me for a Nazi.

Sweat poured down my forehead and stung my eyes. My lungs burned with over-exertion. I was grinding out Black Tiger, Lohan, and Do Pi Crane forms, as much as I could remember, determined to use my secret weapons to defeat my arch-enemy once and for all.

Whenever I was stressed out, I liked to practice my Kung Fu. I'd learned to keep it to myself, since the guys had ribbed me a bit about it the first few times I showed them what I'd been learning. I'd been so excited, but so naive. I'd thought that everyone would fall in love with the magic of Kung Fu, just like me. Now, I lunged into a Lohan Pushing Mountains Far Away stance, and began breathing deeply from my *dan tien*, a technique taught to me by my old Sifu, Glen Po. In my twenties, he'd run the Black Tiger Hung Gar Institute downtown at the corner of King and Barton Street. Before the school shut its doors, I'd earned my brown belt. In his late seventies, Sifu had decided it was finally time to retire. I knew I probably hadn't really earned my brown belt, not in the traditional sense like others had. I mean, I knew that I was never the strongest or most coordinated, but I think I'd impressed Sifu Po with my work ethic and consistent attendance. I rarely missed a class, despite my history of avoidance and procrastination in all things real-world. Once, I'd actually broken a brick with my bare hand. He'd been so proud of me!

A flood of emotions welled up inside me. I missed Sifu Po. He had been really, really good to me.

His soft voice reverberated in my mind, "Relax your muscles, Norbie. If you are stiff and tight, you will be like a kinked garden hose and your chi will not flow." *Yes, Sifu. Thank you so much, Sifu*".

No matter how hard I tried, I couldn't center myself. It had always been hard for me to ignore the nervous thoughts and cartoon fantasies constantly bombarding my brain. And now, with so much at stake, it was impossible.

Frustrated, I dropped to the tarmac and busted out eleven push-ups, then gassed out. My head was throbbing.

Then I jumped up and busted out fifteen inside circle kicks, pretending each one smacked The Screw's head and spun him like a top. The last kick kinked my hip, but I soldiered on, anyway. Then I cranked out seven knuckle push-ups, ignoring the pain as tiny pebbles and broken glass dug into my skin. Then came my pièce de résistance. I had never shown anyone, not even Morag. I did the front splits. Not perfectly, but still, for a guy my age? Awesome! Sifu Po had drilled into me that it's almost impossible to do them again once you age and stiffen, so I had never stopped. If John had seen me, he'd have split his gut!

Exhausted and sweaty, I rested, so, of course, my monkey brain took over. Where was my wife? The longer I waited, the more worried I got. Then I did what I'd been putting off. I read the latest text from Tye:

Just got orders for 500+ copies for
Secret Headquarters, Gold Apple Comics,
And Midtown Comics. You're hitting gold,
man! Ka-ching! Better aim to have
Vol. 2 ready for next month dude!
$$$

Man, the universe was a cruel place. All my dreams were coming true, but right in the middle of a total nightmare.

Then I searched online for trending videos. I found what I'd pretty much expected. A Channel 11 breaking story showing The Screw inside my shop, wielding his gun against John Travolta, Mario Andretti, Steven Dundee and Yosh Schmenge, while cheery Polka music played. A clip of Jimmy-the-Barber puffing a fag as he watched the skinheads and the Rainbow warriors duking it out, turning to the reporter as if speaking to a pub buddy, "Bloody fascists, the lot of them". A police car chasing after The Screw as he tore away in his black muscle car. More police. And my favourite, the white supremacists chanting "Heil Humpty".

Then I checked Donny's YouTube site. He'd launched ten new videos! Hundreds of thousands of new views! I felt sick to my stomach.

Music. I needed music to calm my savage breast. So, I clicked on CKOC's live music icon, and was immediately stunned.

"This one goes out to Hamilton's Village Vigilante, Norbert Reingruber, requested by none other than his old buddy, Steven Dundee!" The DJ played a song by the Animals, "Don't Let Me Be Misunderstood." *Steven knows exactly what I'm going through. He's always known! Like God himself. He's fuzzin' omniscient! I love you, man! Thanks so much for remembering me!*

At that moment, I was wishing that Steven would land a helicopter in the parking lot, saving us all, like 007. I knew *that* Steven was just a figment of Donny's over-active imagination, but it was a nice fantasy. Where the heck *was* Steven, anyway? It was pretty nice to think that he'd been keeping track of me. It was also pretty embarrassing, considering what a fuzzin' sheet-show my life had become.

I nearly jumped out of my skin when I felt a hand on my back.

"Babe, it's me," Morag whispered intensely. She slipped out of the shadow into the dim light like a hot, sexy panther. She carefully pulled me out of my Dragon Tiger pose.

I pitched into her arms and hugged her for a very long time. She fit me perfectly. I realized how much I loved and needed this woman. I was so afraid for her, and for everybody else I knew. *How in blazes was I going to fix this mess?*

"You okay, babe?" She pulled away and gasped. "Your beard! Wow, you look ten years younger."

I probably looked like a baby-faced tween. *Not good*, I thought. *I need to look older, not younger.* But the way my wife was looking at me, maybe I did look better.

"No beard. You're wearing your *gi*. Hmm, pretty sexy, Reingruber. If we weren't in mortal danger..." Morag pulled me in close. We had a really good moment, but then her brain came back online.

"By the way, I saw your costumes and that crazy stunt at the shop. Ugh. That was Donny's idea, wasn't it?"

I tried to explain, but the look on Morag's face wasn't good. I recognized that look. My leg started pumping, all on its own.

"Norbie, don't you see?" she said, urgently, gripping my arms, her eyes wide with fear. She stood on her tippy-toes. "The police haven't caught him. If they *don't* catch him, we're dead. He's intelligent. He'll hunt us down and kill fast. Right now the only safe place is the Club. It's basically a munitions depot, so we have more than enough firepower to defend ourselves. I want you to go back there with me, *now.*"

It ripped me up to see her afraid, and to know that I couldn't make her feel better, and I always wanted to make her feel better.

"Uh, no, honey, it's not safe there," I said. "The police went there to interview everyone. You likely just missed them. They will have shut it all down by now, taken away the guns and stuff. There's no point in going back. Sorry."

Seeing the look on her face, I was desperate to make her feel safe. "But don't you worry, baby! I'm gonna kill that fuzzin' buzz-tard!" I could feel the chi pumping in me. "I will *kill* him. before I let him hurt you!" I grabbed her into a fierce hug. "*Kill* him!" I yelled. "Fuzzin' obliterate!"

Out of the corner of my eye, I noticed the bikers outside the donut shop suddenly stand up, still and alert. They were staring at me as if I'd just threatened to kill *Morag. Think, Norb!* "It's okay, guys, no need to worry. We're just having a hug," I called to them. I released Morag, who was still reeling from me yelling into her ear. She staggered a little. That didn't read well, did it?

Fuzz! The next thing I knew they were on their hogs, throttling towards us. Basically, the leather-clad cavalry had come to save the damsel in distress. Humpty Dumpty was not only a neo-Nazi, he was also a wife-beater. Great.

Chapter 19

I DIDN'T WIMP OUT. I was getting better at this bravery thing.

As soon as the bikers circled us, I performed my Black Tiger form, beginning to end, to show them what they we were up against. During key strikes, I grunted "Kia!", right from the pit of my belly.

The bikers just howled at me.

"What? You jokers find this funny? Do you have any idea who you guys are messing with?" I looked to Morag to see if she was impressed. She look horrified.

A biker, taller and heftier than me, but with a normal-sized head, almost fell off his hog from laughing so darn hard. "Humpty Dumpty, Kung Fu Master? Are you for fucking real?" Lots of guffaws after that one.

I straightened my spine and tried to muster up a final shred of dignity.

Turns out Morag and the big guy recognized each other from the library. His name was Art. He was a huge history buff and a Maine Coon cat owner. Morag had helped him find research on a variety of topics, apparently. After she reassured him, repeatedly, that I wasn't a wife beater, he gave me the stink eye, but then he and his comrades turned around and hogged it back to Hortons for another round of coffee and donuts.

Morag wheeled her pink scooter out from behind the cedar hedge where I normally kept mine. I missed my Vespa. It was probably still lying in Mountain View Park, riddled with bullet holes, like a poor, orange corpse.

Morag cranked her bike to life, and on I hopped. She straddled my lap, backwards. If it had been the other way around, I would have crushed her. Her scooter was smaller than mine, so we had no choice. We must have looked pretty strange.

I buzzed us past the bikers and we waved goodbye to each other like old friends. I swung south onto Steel Street.

At the intersection, Donny's *Making Steven Famous* billboard mocked me. The scooter's engine heaved and sputtered, fighting to stay alive under our weight—well, mostly mine. *Dang!*

"We forgot to wear our helmets!" I shouted above the wind.

"No time for conformity, Norbie!"

"What about your dad? Think The Screw will hunt him down?" Her dad, Mr. Cairnduff, lived out in Digby, Nova Scotia. He was a retired high school teacher. Last year, he'd sold his house and retired there.

"I called him. I'm not sure he believed me, but at least he's on the lookout. And he has his shotgun. He's not exactly the Terminator, but he's a decent shot."

We sputtered along to a McDonald's. The drive-thru was jammed, so we parked in a dark corner of the lot and ran in, bringing our bags of food back out and hunkering back down between two massive pick-up trucks to eat. All the stress of the past few days had amped up our appetites. Morag ate even more than I did. *Morag,* I thought, *always the rebel.* Man, I loved her for that. As she scarfed the last bit of her second Quarter Pounder, my phone rang.

I had a short, choked conversation, my mouth full of fries. "That was Donny. The Screw set fire to their cars in front of that house on Kingslea! Everyone is totally freaking out." Morag's face blanched, and I saw, for the first time ever, huge bags under her eyes. *Had all my stupid ideas finally aged her?*

"Ok, so what's your next move, babe?" she said.

"Donny says to head back to the Tartan Club. The police are gone, and he thinks The Screw still doesn't know anything about it. Tony warned the Dads in time to hide the weapons, so they still have all their firepower."

Morag leapt back up onto my lap.

She was staring hard at me, pressing her face closer to mine. Hostility and determination had edged out the usual sweetness in her face. I braced myself—I'd seen her like this before and that scared me.

"Donny's making a total mockery of you, Norbie! He's posting his bullshit Humpty Dumpty Village Vigilante videos faster than a spinning lottery wheel. How the hell does he find the time to do all that, with so much at stake? Tell me, Norbie, how?" Anger scrunched her face. "Sometimes I think he *is* the fucking devil!" I thought she was going to hit me, but instead, she pressed her warm hand against my chest and melted me.

"What kind of friend manipulates you for his own gain? Ruins *your* life? A real friend wouldn't do that. He's making you look like a total fool, Norbie, so he can get more hits on his Bandcamp page or sell his book. When this is over, if we survive, I need you to take a long break from Donny, for *our* sake. Will you promise me that?"

"He can't help himself," I said, feeling a sudden soft spot for my old friend. "You know what he's like." Even though I had promised myself I would take a long break from Donny only hours earlier, now I felt bad about it. Donny was sick.

"Yes, I do. I know *exactly* what he's like. He's a narcissist. And there's no changing a narcissist." She paused. From experience, I knew she was about to deliver the kicker. "When this is over, and it will be over, I want you to order him to erase those stupid Humpty Dumpty videos and sue him if he doesn't. After that, like I said, you need to take a very long break from Donny Love." She swallowed. "For the sake of our marriage."

My jaw dropped. A strangled little squeak came out of my mouth. To me, it had sounded like Morag had just told me to put Donny in his place or she'd divorce me. *Oh my gawd!* The panic overwhelmed me. I nodded and nodded, afraid to speak.

I yanked my phone out and speed-dialed Donny, but all I got was a message saying his mailbox was full. "Shoot, his mailbox is full!" I said, holding out my phone to Morag like an olive branch. "You heard that, right? Otherwise, I definitely would have left a message." She looked calmer, now.

Determined to show Morag I wasn't a procrastinating ninny, I cranked the engine. "Off to the Club, my lady, as requested." I was about to crank the throttle, when something frightening triggered a deep *knowing* inside me. In the distance, a dark runner of smoke was funnelling up past rooftops into the starless night. Flames shot skyward. All of a sudden, I was six years old and Mutti had just told me the horrible news that Dad had gone to heaven.

Chapter 20

WE CHUGGED INTO MUTTI'S driveway. Fire had turned her garage into Dante's inferno. It spat out roaring flames and dark acrid smoke. Bits of burnt stuff floated down from the sky like volcanic ash.

I'd been wondering if he'd do something this terrible, but now I knew, and the *knowing* was the worst feeling I'd ever had. It was the knowledge of *real* evil.

"That fucking animal!" I cried. In an emergency situation, it was okay to swear. And, besides, Morag didn't put up a fuss.

We bumped off the scooter. It tipped over and crashed against the driveway.

I covered my face with my hands against the punishing heat as I booted to the side of the garage and retrieved the garden hose. I tried to spray water at the fire but it fell short. I moved closer but the heat was unbearable. Morag was on the phone to 911, but I was afraid the whole house would be in flames soon.

Mutti would be devastated.

When shit goes down. Tony's words echoed inside my brain. Shit was definitely going down! Morag rubbed my back as I sprayed water. Mutti's neighbour, Mr. Saunders, had strung his garden hose over the hedge, but gave up after a few punishing minutes. I kept trying, hoping the water would trickle in past the lip of the garage and douse the fire from the ground up, but the flames simply evaporated the water. I scanned the street behind us, desperate for the signs and sounds of fire trucks. "C'mon, you guys, what's taking you so fuzzin' long!"

A couple of teens on bikes rode up to watch. There were cars stopped, and Mutti's neighbours stood on their porches, in their house coats. Some lit up cigarettes and enjoyed a smoke. That was tasteless. One guy enjoyed a beer.

"I'm so sorry, Norbie," Morag said. She was using her forearm to shield her face from the murderous heat. She stifled a sob, doing her best to stay strong for me. She shouted above the sudden din of sirens and the roaring fire. "I'll go tell the cops it was The Screw. Now that the fire trucks are here, back up and let them take over. Just stand over there and rest."

I don't remember agreeing to that, but, according to Morag, I had stood back on the lawn and my life flashed before me like a child's flip book. Childhood memories of when Dad was alive, all the great Sunday family dinners, the great Christmases, the fun German relatives who'd vacationed all summer long at our house, the first time I'd brought Morag home and Mutti had instantly loved her, hanging out in the basement with my friends, playing video games and eating pizza, family trips down to Niagara Falls and Long Point Beach. The fire was severing me from my past, somehow forcing me to finish growing up, whatever that was supposed to look like. It was brutal.

Morag had come back and slipped her arm around my waist. Then we noticed that some of the gathering spectators weren't neighbours. They were Village Vigilante fans, Humpty Dumpty fans! *What the fuzz!*

Someone, *Donny, no fuzzin' doubt,* had tipped them off that their favourite celeb was now also an angry arsonist, perhaps trying to kill his mom by setting her house on fire! Oh, I wanted to throttle Donny *so* bad.

One of the onlookers had an orange Vespa. I saw a couple wearing his and hers t-shirts with pictures of Humpty Dumpy jauntily kicking his heels in mid-air. Underneath, in bold red letters, "*Humpty Dumpty is the Village Vigilante!*" More fans arrived on foot, many wearing last year's Steven t-shirts. The crazy train had definitely arrived! *Thanks, Donny, you fuzzin' hacky sack!*

A couple of crazies raced up the driveway, angling for my autograph, until the heat from the fire forced them back down. Over on the sidewalk, they chanted the lyrics from another of Donny's viral

YouTube songs: "Humpty Dumpty, he's our man, if he can't catch you, nobody can!"

God help me!

"What happened to your beard, Humpty?" a voice shouted over the roaring flames.

"I'm not Humpty!" I roared. "I'm Norbert Reingruber. And I'm trying to save my mom's house from burning down. So why don't you cut the bullshit and lend a fucking hand?"

But, in their world, I was Humpty, and I fought criminals, not fires. They couldn't let me escape the box they'd locked me in, just like my old friends couldn't, or wouldn't. They stared at me as if I'd asked them to help me build a spaceship out of hair.

By now, a fire truck had tried to pull in front of the house, but they were having trouble getting all the crazies and their vehicles out of the way.

"Hey, guys, look! Humpty's a Kung Fu warrior, too!" yelled a skinny acolyte over the roaring flames. "How cool is that!" He was wearing a skin-tight t-shirt. In shock, I realized that my face was on his shirt! And not even a nice photo. I looked like I'd be at home carrying a bloody axe.

I suddenly felt like a fool for wearing my *gi* in public.

"You're so awesome!" cried another guy. He hoisted his cellphone over his head, snapped photos of me, then tapped the screen, no doubt posting the photos online.

Then something even more insane happened. A white van skidded to a stop in front of the house. The side door slid open and out jumped four Humpty Dumptys, complete with white pancake make-up, humongous egg-heads, bright red tights and tiny red bowler caps. It was as if each one of them had literally popped off the original potato chip bag. They began to dash towards me, waving their arms excitedly.

"What the heck is wrong with you people? Get away from me!" I started running away from them, in a bizarre chase around Mutti's front lawn. I felt violated.

"Leave my husband alone, you freaks!" Morag shrieked. She went into attack mode, chasing after the slowest egg man.

"Morag," I yelled, craning my neck at the scene behind me, "don't!" Phone cameras flashed.

Unfortunately for him, that Dumpty was not very fast on his feet. My wife tackled him and took him down hard. The crowd uttered a collective "Owww."

"Never *ever* chase my husband again. Understand?" she said, inches from his face.

"Yes, yes, ma'am," he stuttered. "Sorry."

Morag growled a little. "Mmm. Okay. Now get outta here." She stood up and gave him a jerk with her thumb.

The crowd cheered. "Let's hear it for Mrs. Humpty!" someone cried. Morag looked nauseated at that one.

"You're amazing, Humpty!" a fan cried, "You're a real Hammer Hero."

"We love you V.V.!" another Dumpty yelled. There was a chorus of "We love you" from the other nutbars.

"You really are our hero," another said. "We love you!"

Finally, the firefighters had managed to get a hydrant. A powerful gush of fire-killing water arced past me.

I was so relieved I began to cry. Maybe the rest of Mutti's house would survive, after all. But, even with the firefighters dousing the flames, I realized their efforts were likely in vain. The garage was utterly destroyed, and I was pretty certain the flames were burning through the wall separating Mutti's house. I was heart-broken and scared.

By midnight, police had managed to cordon off Mutti's property. The gawkers and their vehicles had been pushed back. But the News trucks had arrived. They were interviewing anyone with a pulse.

Reporters and camera crew grabbed the weirdos and gave them a moment of fame.

Someone tapped me on the shoulder. An autograph hound, even nerdier-looking than me, held out a marker and an orange Humpty t-shirt. "I'd be truly honoured if you'd sign it, V.V. I really admire your work."

An awful rage boiled inside me. I fantasized about throwing the guy into the garage-furnace, so he'd learn a hard lesson about respecting people's privacy. At the look on my face, he wisely forgot about the autograph and slunk off.

My dark fantasy made me realize just how super-scared and angry I truly was. *Please God, don't let me turn into an angry Nazi. I'm just a good German boy.* That's what Mutti used to tell me when I was little, and I wanted to stay that way.

Chapter 21

MORAG UNDERSTOOD PEOPLE, way more than I ever did.

She cupped her hands around her mouth, stood on her tippy-toes, and shouted at the top of her lungs, "Humpty has a wicked case of diarrhea, folks! I'm taking him home to use the toilet. We'll be back in a jiff!" She gave a cheery smile to a police officer who grimaced at her.

Hearing I had diarrhea crinkled a few noses. They looked disappointed. *Good,* I thought. *It's about time.*

"Awesome idea, Morag!" I whispered.

"Whatever," she said as she righted her scooter.

I hopped on. She straddled me, and I didn't care anymore how that looked. I fired up the pink bugger and chugged it past my "fans". We throttled north towards our apartment, the engine heaving. We were travelling as fast as a geriatric jogger.

"At Flux," Morag said, "turn right and swing along Argon Avenue to Iron Street."

"Will do!"

Morag's quick thinking had outsmarted the lookie-loos. She had us faking need for a bathroom and carving a route back to the safety of the Tartan Club. *Brilliant!*

All that time I'd been hosing the fire, I couldn't shake the fear that The Screw was already at the Club, shooting everyone like fish in a barrel.

Approaching a red light, we pulled alongside the Route 21 bus. Two skinheads sitting by the window noticed me and excitedly banged on the window, shooting me Nazi salutes.

"Leave me alone, bumheads!" I gave them the finger.

They looked really hurt. And I just didn't care. If you had told me a few days ago that I'd be ready to get into it with killer dwarves and neo-Nazis, I would have thought you were crazy. Yet, here I was.

Soon we were booting east on Iron Street and then south onto the long road that was good ol' Kingslea Drive. I glanced over my shoulder and saw we weren't being followed. Huge relief, let me tell you.

The engine of the little scooter was sounding worse, and I was convinced it would soon conk.

We passed the Incognito House and the elementary school. I was suddenly struck with a deep hunger. I spoke without thinking. "Morag, wanna grab a sub before we hit the Club?"

She stared at me like I'd suggested skydiving without a parachute. "Are you for real, buddy? At a time like this!"

"Don't listen to me. You know I don't make sense when I'm stressed out." I sighed. One of my favourite things to do was boot across the street to Mike's Submarine Shop and order a torpedo with all the fixings and extra sub-sauce, of course. I swear I'd single-handedly kept their business afloat. Anyway, our McDonald's feast had been only a couple of hours ago. I knew I probably wasn't *really* hungry.

We slugged up to the end of Kingslea and along Moxley Drive, and then the engine did, in fact, conk out. We coasted to a stop against the curb. Up ahead, on our right, was the Blue Fountain apartment building. It'd been there forever.

"Arg!" Morag groaned. "I meant to fill it up yesterday! Shit."

"It's okay. We'll figure something out."

She hopped off my lap and paced.

My mind raced with possible solutions to our problem. "Let's take the Sludge Road bus. It'll give us time to devise a new plan. I mean, we don't have a *specific* plan, so that's a huge problem, right? The Screw has a *specific* plan to kill everyone, so we should have one, too."

"The *bus*, Norbie? Are you frickin' kidding me! What if The Screw's already at the Club? By the time we get there, everyone could be dead!"

My face flushed. "Okay, I'm paralyzed by fear *again*, I get it. You're right, call us a cab."

While we waited, she started pacing again. "I appreciate your effort, Norbie, I really do, although as usual, you're very misguided. You're a good man, and you have a good heart and you mean well, but..."

"But what?"

Tears glistened in her eyes. She swallowed a lump in her throat, and lowered her voice to a tender whisper. "You need to face your fears in the moment, Norb. You can't keep putting them off. You know we don't have time to catch a bus, or grab a sub, not with so much at stake, but you went there. And you won't properly manage Tank and Harlan because you're *afraid* they won't like you."

I nodded. She was right. She was always right.

"It's okay to be afraid, babe. It's normal."

"I'm *so* sorry, Morag. I know I have a serious problem. And, until now, I didn't realize just how badly it's affected you. I promise, from the bottom of my pathetic, fearful heart, I will change. I *am* changing. I can feel it! I can't lose you. You're everything to me."

She bit her lip and blinked back her tears.

I opened my mouth but nothing came out but a pathetic squeak. I had nothing left inside me to convince my wife I'd face my fears. For once, I was out of excuses.

"And another thing," Morag said.

"Yeah?"

"We don't need a specific plan."

"We don't?"

"Nope."

"Why not?

She stared up into the night sky.

I'd never seen her so outside of herself, so vulnerable.

"Morag, what is going on here? Why on God's green earth don't we need a specific plan?"

"Because there's already a plan brewing at the Tartan Club. God help us all."

Chapter 22

In the back of the cab, my phone rang like crazy. First, some guy named Damien, his voice low like a vacuum cleaner, offered me ten grand to assassinate a kid who'd bullied him more than forty years ago in Grade Eight. A crazed-sounding woman wanted me to track down the thief who'd stolen her car out of her driveway, torture him—*yikes!*—and *then* turn him over to the police. It all got worse from there. At one a.m., I stopped answering the phone or listening to voicemail messages.

Donny's stupid picture came up on my call display, but I was afraid of what I'd say to him in my current emotional state, so I let the call go to voice mail. Tye Novak had left an earlier message, but he was blethering so fast I couldn't make out a single word. My jaw tightened, cinched, tightened. The worst call was from the police. I actually pretended they had the wrong number and hung up. I was *that* anxious. They tried again but I ignored them. *Avoidance*, I thought. *Same as procrastination.* I peeked over at Morag. But what was I supposed to do? I didn't have time to chat with the police or anybody else. I had to save everyone! I tried to wring my phantom beard, forgetting it had been lopped off by Patricia. I wrung my hands, but that just wasn't as soothing.

"Turn off your phone," Morag said, taking my hand. "We'll deal with all that crap later."

I turned off the volume, *feeling* as if I'd turned it off.

I squeezed her hand, and she squeezed back.

"I love you, Morag."

She sighed.

She didn't say she loved me. I was crestfallen, but felt a little hopeful knowing she was at least willing to hold hands.

"I'm sorry about procrastinating."

"I know you are, Norbie."

"What about your job?" I said. "You're going to have to miss more work because of all this."

"I have sick days. So I'm good."

"Right. Of course."

Morag ordered the driver to drop us off on Limeridge Road. We re-traced the path that ran between backyards and snaked down to the Tartan Club.

We ran hard until I bonked. From then on we speed-walked, although Morag had to constantly slow for me to catch up. She wasn't usually frustrated by my size and poor physical shape but tonight she couldn't hide her disappointment and had to fight against rolling her eyes at me.

"Morag, what would I do without you?" I said, panting.

Neither of us had to say the answer to *that* one out loud.

My cell phone buzzed in my hand. It was Tank, asking whether to open the store tomorrow.

"No thanks," I said. I lowered my voice and spoke with authority, like a *real* manager, "we still have our major health and safety problems so the shop is closed until further notice. Stay home and stay safe, OK? I'll notify you as soon as we re-open." I decided to call Harlan, to make sure he knew to stay away. I got his voicemail, since it was so late. I made it quick, then added: "Harlan, I wish you the best of luck with your legal battles. You deserve a good outcome". After I hung up, I felt this pleasant stab of self-respect. I hoped Morag was proud of me. *I* was proud of me, and that was saying something, considering I was rarely proud of me. I looked at her hopefully, and saw traces of a little smile on her face, but then she got back to business, yanking me along the path.

"We've gotta keep moving, Norbie!" Shadows and light played across her face. One minute she was an angel, the next a drill sergeant.

"Morag, what if Mutti dies and I'm not there to say goodbye?" I said, breathless. "I won't be able to live with myself."

"Karl's with her, Norbie. He loves her, and she loves him. And she's in a very good hospital with very good care. And she's not going to die today or tomorrow. She's just going through a rough patch. So hang in there, okay? We'll see her when all this is over. I promise."

My knotted thoughts unravelled hard and fast. I could barely pump out the words. "How did writing a stupid comic book turn into such an awful nightmare? I never wanted to be famous, I just wanted to write comic books for people to enjoy. Maybe I should have stuck *The Steel Avenger* in a drawer. I mean, what's the point, anyway? Where's the joy in any of this?"

Morag shook her head, perplexed. "That's life, Norbie. Always a fly in the ointment. But we really can't think about that right now. We have to focus on the present, okay?"

I grabbed onto Morag's words like a lifeline. "Yeah, you're right. We're going to save our loved ones. Focus, Norbie. Forget Humpty. Forget The Screw. Forget the Village Vigilante." I felt myself start to hyper-ventilate. "Forget the fire destroying Mutti's garage and probably her house. Forget that you have a lunatic fan base. Forget that your business is barely breaking even. Forget that your good friend Donny betrayed you. Forget that Tye Novak's a nutter, and that you should have submitted your comic book elsewhere and not taken his offer so hastily." Now I was almost yelling. "Forget you're a stupid loser who will never grow up because you chose to work in a stupid fantasy world where you make stupid money, and your wife makes the real money and will probably never respect you again after everything you've done to her and everybody else!"

A dog barked in the backyard beside us.

"Norbie!" Morag shouted. She turned to me and slapped my cheek. "Focus, man! Get a grip! None of that negative crap in your mind is helpful." She grabbed the collar of my *gi*. "Stay strong, babe. You *can* do this!"

She grabbed my hand and dragged me like a stubborn toddler.

My brain was churning. I thought about the terrible fire and how it had destroyed the hockey cards my dad had bought for my tenth birthday, how they'd help me to cope with Dad's death, how much comfort they'd given me through some of my lonely teenage years. I realized how much I had loved my childhood home, how lucky I was to have grown up with loving parents and friends in the tough but familiar Village, how, after Dad's death, Mutti and I had become a team, in big and little ways. We'd gone grocery shopping together, and I'd done the outside chores, like mowing the lawn and shovelling snow. She'd totally thrilled me on my sixteenth birthday when she'd bought me an *authorized* Neil Peart drum set, and I remembered, with a powerful thumping of my heart, the first time I'd taken Morag home to meet Mutti and Mutti's eyes had twinkled with real delight. They'd *actually* twinkled. She'd been so happy for me. I'd never, ever forget that day. I pawed at my tearful eyes. Morag saw my sadness, but that only tightened her resolve. She was obviously determined to complete our mission tonight before giving into her own emotions regarding *my* emotions. *Man*, she was so tough.

All of a sudden, my love for Morag pumped my heart to Superman proportions. I vowed to stop The Screw's reign of terror and see that he spent the rest of his life behind bars. And then I'd hammer Donny with an ultimatum, and, if he didn't meet my demands, I'd shut him down for at least a year. *And* I'd blow up my fearful ways for good, so Morag would always respect me. I wasn't sure exactly when my flaw had taken root. Somewhere in childhood, I guessed. Regardless, it was a huge problem now, and I had to fix it before Morag fuzzin' divorced me, or popped a bullet in my skull, which might be preferrable.

Maybe there was a support group I could join and attend weekly meetings. Donny had told us he'd tried to form a group called LA:

Liars Anonymous. Apparently, there'd been little interest so he'd abandoned the idea. Now I wondered if he'd lied about that. I doubted there was a Procrastinators Anonymous, or ManBoys Anonymous, or whatever it was I needed, but I'd definitely book a few sessions with a shrink.

Twenty minutes later, at the bottom of the hill, we found ourselves shrouded in darkness. I flicked on my Batman pen light and pointed it low to the ground. The Tartan Club was visible now, through the trees.

Mud Creek gurgled and there was a chorus of peepers.

Suddenly, there was one other sound, coming from the Tartan Club, it was horrendous, wince-inducing, like hearing fingernails dragged hard along a chalkboard.

A light above the rear bay door sputtered, then took hold. It had an unfamiliar reddish glow.

We tapped off our phone lights and surreptitiously made our way to the back door, scanning the parking lot and shrubbery for signs of The Screw. My heart was pounding in my ears.

The closer we got to the club, the louder the terrible whining sound became.

Something was really wrong here.

"I don't like this, Norbie!" Morag hissed. "What's that sound? It's horrible!" She had her hands over her ears.

Chills were crawling up my spine. "I think we should run," I whispered.

"What?" she said.

"Run!" I mouthed at her.

So we did, awkwardly, with our hands at our ears.

As we neared the Club, it dawned on me that the light above the door was in fact a giant red neon bagpipe! Morag and I stared at each other in disbelief. "What the heck, Mr. Love," I whispered. "You just put a target on our heads? You idiot Scottish nationalist bumhead!"

We frantically banged on the door, peering over our shoulders.

"Call Donny, get him to open the door!"

In our panic, we'd forgotten to call.

Just as I pulled out my phone, Donny whipped open the door, hustled us inside, and locked the door behind us.

I was about to breath a huge sigh of relief.

And that's when I realized the shocking sound we'd heard outside was, in fact, the screeching of the agony bags, as Donny only half-jokingly called them.

My patience blew out the door. But it was Morag who said it. "What the fuck?"

And I didn't even get after her for swearing. I figured I owed her.

Chapter 23

THROUGH THE KITCHEN serving window, we glimpsed the ludicrous.

Mr. Love, Mr. Valentini, and Mr. Pappas had joined arms and were swaying drunkenly to the ear-piercing wail of bagpipes as the P.A. blasted a recording of "Scotland the Brave".

The Dads had scrounged up faded army fatigues and helmets, but for some reason had forgone army boots in favour of dress shoes, and, in Mr. Love's case, an old pair of velcro running shoes.

The only blessing was that the tv in the corner had been turned off, so at least we didn't have to listen to Captain Crunch dishing up late-breaking news about the adventures of Humpty Dumpty and the Village Vigilante.

Shaking with anger, I pounded into the hall. The women were slumped at one of many circular tables, dressed in fatigues and surrounded by empty beer cans.

"What the heck is going on here!" I shouted. "Is this how we protect ourselves from The Screw? By getting drunk?"

The men blinked at me.

Angela belched and took another slug. She looked exhausted and haggard. Anger had squeezed Allison's face into a tight fist, an expression usually reserved for her husband, Donny. She was drunkenly rocking Stewart in her arms, trying to soothe him, but he kept bawling, exhausted and overloaded by the wailing bagpipes. Morag marched over to the P.A. system and shut the music off. The silence was beautiful.

"Hey," said Mr. Love, "we were listening tae that!" He pointed an accusatory finger at me. "You're no' going to tell *me* what to do, Norbert Reingruber!" The other two men blinked at me, trying to remember how they knew me.

Mr. Love ranted some more. "You're no' man enough to fight in a war! All those years living in your mama's basement have stunted ya." He looked over at Mrs. Love. "You were right, Esme. This lad is permanently stunted!" He shifted his gaze back at me. "Go join the Girl Scouts of Canada, ya wee girl!" He scoffed. "Eff they'll even have ya!"

"Shut it, Dad!" Donny snapped.

Mr. Love shook a fist at Donny. "You're never too old for a good tannin', lad. Remember that!"

"Right back at you, *old man*." Donny adjusted his cowboy hat. He was still rockin' Clint Eastwood Steven Dundee. His make-up was badly smeared.

Tony sat beside Angela and eight-year-old Angelina, gnawing his index finger, deep in thought. He was way angrier than usual. When Tony's angry, look out. I wondered how he had let things get so out of control here. Maybe he was mad at himself.

For once, John was quiet and reserved. He'd crossed his legs, and was just observing, mentally taking notes, nodding at intervals.

Why had these guys let the Dads go crazy like this? Jeez, what about the little kids? Did no one know how to act like a grown-up anymore?

Ironically, Donny had somehow parachuted out of his mania. The fire in his eyes had cooled. He was quiet. Maybe, between him and me, we could talk some sense into everyone else now.

"Mr. Love," I said, finally. "I'm not as stunted as you think, and I'm not in Grade Three anymore, so I have no idea why you keep treating me like I am. And if no one here is going to be sensible, then, yes, I *will* tell you what to do."

"Oh dear," said Mrs. Love, puffing on her fag, "you look a bit like Bruce Lee, if he were a chubby German boy. That's a kung fu outfit, right?"

I nodded.

"Ach," said Mr. Love, "you wouldn't know kung fu from your arse!" He bristled. "Look at the lot of you. Aye, a bunch of fuckin' pansies playing dress-up. And look at Donny, pretending to be Steven Dundee. Utterly pathetic. You know what's wrong with this generation? Too much time wanking off on the World Wide Web." He put on his best whiny voice. "Who am I? What am I? Ooo, I don't know! Ooo, I'm so sensitive! What a load of utter shite!"

"Cool it, Archie," said Mrs. Love, "you're no' right in the *heed*." She blew an impressive smoke ring.

"You should talk, nutter!"

I shut my mouth—there was no changing Mr. Love's mind on most things, and now was definitely not the time to try. He was unlike anyone else I knew; he didn't give a damn what people thought of him and said whatever was on his mind. I kind of admired that. I, on the other hand, was afraid of what everyone thought of me. Somehow, I had to fix that.

"Look, anything that could draw his attention here is a *huge* mistake," I said to all the drunken people in the room. "Like loud music," and I looked pointedly at Mr. Love, "or bright neon lights," and I looked significantly at Donny, who ran to turn off the bagpipe sign.

"I'm really sorry about all of this," Tony growled, leaning toward Morag and me. "These old bastards polished off an entire case of McEwan's. I tried to stop them but Donny's dad flew into a wicked rage. He had stashed six cases under the stage for 'emergencies.'"

"Emergencies?" Morag said. "Well, it's certainly helping with this one." We stared as Mr. Pappas slowly sank to the floor and lay down for a nap.

Morag crossed her arms against her chest. "Why are you fools drinking and dancing when people's lives are at stake? This isn't a joke!"

"Hey, John, go wake up your dad, and let's try to get these guys sobered up," I said.

"Gee, glad you're here to rescue us, Eggie," John said, his voice cold and smooth. He jiggled his leg. "So do tell, Norb, what *are* next steps? What genius plan do you have in that big head of yours?"

I felt my anger rising.

Even after all the kerfuffle at the shop, John was still dressed impeccably, not a single hair or piece of clothing out of place. Had he gone home and changed? Had he even tried to get things under control here?

"Cool it, John," Morag warned.

He raised an eyebrow. She had never been anything but nice to him.

I had no time for John's bull crap. I had a war to win.

Tony had joined us for the war council. "Look, our Dads are insane. They won't listen to reason, and they're liquored right up."

We all had another look. Mr. Valentini was staring at the floor, swaying dangerously. Mr. Pappas was having a noisy sleep, and Mr. Love was still half-dancing to the music in his head.

"At least they're not arguing anymore." Tony took a long, deep swig of beer and swiped at his damp forehead.

"We need to get everyone organized, now that we're all here," Donny said, returning.

"Troops! Man your posts!" he yelled.

There was a shifting and a little bit of kerfuffle, but within a few minutes, the hall was quiet and empty, except for us five.

"Where'd they go?" I asked.

"Oh, various assignments," Donny said vaguely. "Like lookout duty."

"Lookout duty?"

"Yeah, don't worry about it. I got it all figured out."

"Wow, okay." For once, maybe Donny *did* actually have it figured out. I was impressed with him, although I had trouble admitting that to myself. I took a moment to really look around the hall.

Then my heart began to race. At the four windows, two on each side of the hall, ancient-looking machine guns on tripods had been perched on tables tucked in behind the old curtains. Under each table there was a green metal crate overflowing with ammunition belts. On the north side of the hall, Allison and Mr. Pappas each manned their machine gun; on the south side, Mr. Valentini and Donny. With war imminent, the old boys had suddenly sobered up. *Wow!*

Mrs. Love was gently rocking Stewart, her fag dangling from her lip. The poor kid had finally fallen asleep. We wouldn't need to call Children's Aid, after all. She canted slightly because of her bum knee, but otherwise stood as if calmly waiting with her grandson at a bus stop.

"Donny," I squeaked. "Where did they get all the guns and ammunition?"

"Oh my God!" Morag said, surveying the machine guns and ammunition, her eyes growing to the size of saucers. "Is everyone insane? We're facing four men armed with *pistols*, not an entire army, for Pete's sake!"

"More will come," Mr. Love shouted. "They always do!"

"Follow me," Tony said to Morag and me. He exhaled slowly. "There's something I need to show you. And try not to freak out, okay?"

"Right, hen," Mr. Love called out to Morag, "you and the other girls get down into the bunker. Women aren't cut out for war, that's a known fact."

Mrs. Love scoffed. "Shut it, chauvinist pig!" Stewart stirred in her arms, then settled again.

Allison and Angela ignored Mr. Love.

Morag's face turned fire-engine red. I knew that she was about to tear a strip off of Mr. Love for his blatant sexism, but I wordlessly begged her not to. She knew this wasn't the time to pick a fight with the old fool.

Angela had turned from her machine gun. I was startled to see she'd started smoking again, after having quit cold turkey ten years ago. "Tone," she said, as we passed her. "FYI, I'm not some brainwashed woman from 1952. I have dreams of having a real career, just like you had dreams of being a race car driver. Next year, I'm going back to school and getting a degree in education. I'm going to be an elementary school teacher. And if you don't like it, too bad for you."

Tony's face dropped. "You're telling me this *now*? Here?"

"Yeah." She folded her arms across her chest.

"Fuck me," Tony said. He threw his hands up into the air. "Okay, you want to be a teacher. Fine, no problem. Mama fucking mia."

Shaking his head, he led us through a side door and down a set of rusted steel stairs to the basement, which was practically a tomb. John trailed us, as if he had nothing better to do. He didn't utter a single smart remark. I figured he'd taken Morag's warning seriously.

At the bottom of the stairs, Tony heaved against a heavy steel door. "Give me a hand, Norb."

Very slowly, it gave way, groaning and squealing.

A wave of damp, musty air squared us in the face.

Tony flicked on a light switch. In a huge room, half the size of the main floor, there were stacks of munition boxes, rows of Vickers machine guns with pre-fed ammunition belts, and Mills bomb hand grenades. Enough to blow up the Club a hundred times over! In between the stacks of death, on the walls, were cheery photos of people dancing and partying at the club throughout the years. There was also one very saucy picture of a scantily-clad Sheena Easton.

"What is this?" I croaked.

"It's an actual bunker. Walls are frickin' three feet thick. Mr. Love and his old war comrades built it in the Fifties. Turns out he was a munitions expert. Scary, right?" Tony shook his head. "Guess the Scots wanted a safe place to hide in case World War Three broke out." He stared at me, sighed heavily. "These last few hours have been shit, Norb.

It was like being stuck in *The Dirty Dozen*. Turns out *all* our Dads know a guy who *knows* a guy, and they had them truck in all this old-school artillery, which, apparently, still works. The whole time the girls were freaking out, and those old stubborn bastards wouldn't listen to them, or me. After a while, I just gave up. They'd obviously made up their minds." Tony made a strange face. "The old buggers really teamed up. If we weren't all going to die, I'd be happy for them."

"Okay," Morag said, "I've heard enough. We're calling the cops. These old fools are definitely going to get us all killed."

"Morag's right," I said. "This has gotten way out of hand. What if we *actually* kill one of the bad guys? What if *we* end up going to jail and not them!"

"Everyone we know and love is here with us," Morag said. "So calling the cops won't endanger anyone on the outside. In case you two haven't noticed, we're sitting ducks stuck in a cinder block with a bunch of drunken war veterans who couldn't fire a pea out a pea shooter, if their lives depended on it. For heaven's sake, you and Donny have *children* here, Tony. This stops now."

"Be my guest, Morag," Tony said. "Call the cops." He looked from Morag to me. "But The Screw doesn't know we're here, right?"

Morag and I traded glances.

"No," I said. "Probably," Morag said at the exact same moment.

"What?" I yelped.

"I just assumed he did," she said. "He seems pretty smart to me. He'd have someone check on where the police went to do their interviews after the fiasco at the shop."

Shoot! I hadn't thought of that.

Morag's lower lip began to tremble. Her fears were getting to her, to all of us. She eyed the doorway as if expecting The Screw to make a cameo appearance.

I tore my phone out of my pocket. "I'm calling the police! Screw The Screw! This is the final showdown. And he doesn't get a say *if* and *when* I call the cops."

I punched in 9-1-1.

It rang only once, before the sound of machine gun fire startled me so badly I dropped the phone. It bounced off the floor, landed, and spun to a stop. Tony raced back up the stairs. John just gaped at me, bewildered-looking.

Morag picked up the phone and finished the call for me. Twin flames burned behind her eyes.

Chapter 24

I DIDN'T BELIEVE IN fighting or any of that patriarchal, macho war stuff. For most of my adult life, I'd viewed myself as an easy-going, kung fu pacifist, and prided myself on *trying* to be a good husband and son. Sometimes, without thinking it through, I considered myself a bit of a humanitarian, just like my idol and almost-best friend Steven Dundee, but on a much smaller scale, of course, but all that self-identity crap flushed down the proverbial crapper as soon as I heard the *rat-a-tat-tat* of machine gun fire from above. Because, with great power comes great responsibility, right? Even at one-thirty in the morning.

So, just like that, I transformed myself, like Dick Grayson did when he became Nightwing.

I bolted up the stairs past Mrs. Pappas, who was now rushing down the stairs towards the safety of the bunker. Mrs. Valentini gripped Angelina's hand and led her to safety. "Good luck!" they called to me.

At the top of the stairs, I rocketed right and through the side door into the darkness of the dance floor, upending myself on table and chairs I could barely see. I sprang back up onto my feet lickety-split, as only Nightwing could!

I half-expected to see the Evil Dead crawling through the shattered windows and chewing on our friends. Thankfully, there were zero demons.

The sharp smell of cordite burned my nostrils.

The only light in the hall came from the red glow of the exit signs. Allison and Mr. Pappas were dimly silhouetted in crimson as they blasted their machine guns. Bullets from outside whizzed past my head and blew out chunks of wall.

Donny and Mr. Valentini had hunkered down beneath their respective windows, drapes drawn, intermittently spraying circular rounds from their guns, then ducking for cover. Shells scattered to the floor in a constant metallic dance.

"Right, Norbie!" Mr. Love cried from the stage. "Get your arse over here!" It was hard to make him out in the darkness. Before I knew it, I was in front of him and he was shoving a Luger into my hand, the same gun my dad had stashed in the family basement. "Defend the front and back doors. Go where you're most needed. You'll need cartridges, lad." He shone a flashlight against a table and nodded at me. "Fill your boots, Norbie! Morag, Tony, get over here!"

I nodded nervously and ran over to the table to grab cartridges. Shoot! I didn't have any pockets in my *gi!* Improvising, I took off my jacket and wrapped it around my waist like a giant fanny pack, stuffing it with ammo. My bare chest and belly were cold, but what choice did I have? I squeezed a helmet on my head and wondered if it would actually stop a bullet.

The Luger felt cold and solid in my hands. Instead of filling me with dread, as I'd expected, it filled me with incredible power. And hope. *Save Morag. Save Mutti. Save everyone!*

Morag and Tony had arrived on the little stage.

"Morag," Mr. Love cried, "you're with Angela at the front door." I guess he'd changed his mind about women and war.

My wife gave me the once-over. I thought I caught just a tiny bit of, you know, *interest* in her look. I think the bare chest and soldier's helmet were kind of turning her on, despite our problems.

Morag took a Luger and a box of ammunition. She gave me a half-smile and headed off.

Mr. Love scrunched up his face. "Tony, take two o' these hand grenades to each position. Handle with care, mind you!"

Tony looked less than grateful to be given this task. He bent double to avoid gunfire and shuffled back and forth with the little balls of death.

"Johnny Pappas!" Mr. Love yelled. "Get off your fancy-pants arse and man the back entrance!"

As if startled from a deep sleep, John jerked to his feet from the corner where he'd hunkered down and half-ran, half-danced to retrieve his Luger from Archie then headed for the back entrance. Nervous reaction, I figured. I was pretty sure he'd rather be back at the family restaurant waiting tables than killing strangers in the dark.

"We will never surrender!" Mr. Love cried, channeling Winston Churchill from the stage. "Good will alway triumph over evil!"

I saw Mrs. Love standing at the doorway to the basement, rocking Stewart. She was crying. Finally, as if satisfied, she turned on her bum leg and disappeared back down towards the safety of the concrete bunker. I didn't know how safe she and Mrs. Pappas and Mrs. Valentini and the kids would be down there, with all that live ammunition. Hopefully, she'd lock the heavy door, in case The Screw came a-knockin'. But, even if he did, I doubted he had enough firepower to penetrate a bunker that looked like it had been built to withstand Armageddon.

Go where you're most needed. I tightened my grip on my Luger. *Who should I help? Allison?* She was firing up a storm. She didn't need my help. She was amazing. Fearless! I was shocked when she spun around and said, "Norbie, take over! My shoulder's numb."

"Me?" *But I'm a Luger guy,* I thought, *not RoboCop.*

Like a ninja, she dove away from the table and shimmied along the floor on her belly.

I crawled over to the table, my heart thumping. I set my Luger on the floor, reached up and squeezed the machine gun's trigger, spraying bullets out the window. It was easier than I thought it'd be. I prayed the police showed up soon. *With all the noise, why the fuzz hadn't they?*

Through sheer force of will, I stood so I could see where I was firing.

I saw a Black Escalade in the front lot. I aimed and fired, metallic pings filling the air.

Thugs leaned out from behind the SUV and fired back. Now I was shooting at people! Shite had just got real, and I did not like it.

Bullets sailed past my head. Allison shoved me away from the gun. "Argh! Just never mind! I'll do it. Use your Luger, Norbie!"

Her muscles now functional, she swung her machine gun, spraying bullets in pulsating arcs, most of them striking the vehicle, sounding like metallic popcorn. I edged the Luger through the window and fired, hoping I'd wounded but not killed someone. I was afraid to show my big head again, as surely this time they wouldn't miss. The bravado I'd felt behind the machine gun dissipated. But, despite that, I raised my head and blew out a headlight. "Holy crap!" I cried. "I did it! I did it!"

"Take that, you fuckers!" Allison cried. *Rat-a-tat-tat!*

Suddenly, at least fifteen shadowy figures dove out from behind the SUV and raced towards the Club. *Holy crap, we're outnumbered!* What kind of crazies would continue an assault on a fortress of machine guns, armed only with hand guns?

"Take that you, you bastards!" Mr. Pappas roared. He ripped out a grenade pin with his teeth and hurled it through the window. Two seconds later, there was a deafening explosion, followed by terrible screams. Mr. Pappas laughed maniacally. Surely, those guys would give up now?

Shivers ran down my spine. Dear Jesus, had Mr. Pappas just killed somebody?

This was all so out of hand. The hint of an awesome plan began to boil up inside my heated brain. I shouted through the window, my voice well above the roar of the gunfire.

"I surrender, Screw! If you stop shooting, I'll come out peacefully. But you have to promise to leave everyone else alone. All of them! This can only be between you and me. Understood?"

"Hold your fire, boys!" The Screw's voice penetrated the darkness.

All at once, the gunfire ceased.

"So, the fuck-up wants to make a deal," he laughed. It was not a nice sound.

My heart was racing. "Do we have a deal?"

"Norb, you've got ten seconds to show your fat, ugly face out here or we'll blow this piece of shit club to Kingdom fucking Come."

"I said, do we have a deal?"

"Sure, we have a deal." You could hear the lie in his voice.

A wail of sirens pierced the darkness. The police were coming, finally. Thank God! The Clash wailed, "Should I Stay or Should I Go Now" through my brain. *What a fuzzin' time to hear that song in my head! Go away, Joe Strummer!*

Morag and the rest of the Tartan Club crew had crawled over to me.

"Norbie, don't you dare!" Morag hissed at me. "It's a trick."

I looked at her helplessly. "I'm taking action. No more procrastinating. Anyway, I knew it was likely a trick. I was just doing what had to be done."

Morag looked sick. "I didn't mean for you to risk your life. To do *this*." She started to cry.

I gave her a kiss on the lips. "You deserve to be married to a man, not a boy. To a hero, not a coward."

Before she could lay her hands on me, I climbed through the window.

As soon as my feet hit the ground, shadowy figures threw a sack over my head and bundled me into the back of the Escalade. They shoved in against me, heavy as cement. Next thing I knew, the SUV was charging out of the parking lot onto Mount Albion Road, roaring in the opposite direction of the approaching sirens.

The thugs stank of B.O. I was so hot and claustrophobic, I thought I would barf. Runners of sweat washed down my forehead and stung my eyes, making me blink.

I realized with sudden clarity that, although I'd made this sacrifice to save everybody, I didn't actually *want* to die. I was hoping for some magical, last-minute rescue, comic-book style.

Sifu Po's words echoed inside my head: *A warrior is already dead. Fight as if you're already dead.*

I tried super-hard to breathe from my *dan tien* to calm and center myself, but there were billions of fearful thoughts zooming inside my head. Then I shouted at myself, inside my head, of course, that I really was a kung fu warrior, and when the time was right I'd pretend I was dead, just like Sifu Po had taught me, and maybe, just maybe, I'd forget about myself long enough to beat the fuzzin' crap out of these over-sized *chalksuckers* and their *craphole* boss.

It was hard to sit still and do nothing, knowing I was on my way to a horrible death that surely involved torture. I imagined Mutti, alone and dying at the hospital. I imagined crying out her name, too late.

I struggled against my handcuffs, but they only cut more. The pain was excruciating. The heat inside the sackcloth was unbearable. My gorge rose. "I can't breathe! I'm going to barf!" I yelled at my captors.

A thug punched my forehead, driving me back against the seat. I swallowed against the exploding pain, and the need to barf. An anger, unlike anything I'd ever experienced, hardened my resolve like fast-cooling steel. Suddenly, I found I could push back on my rising gorge.

I hunkered down. These guys were going to be sorry. Somehow. Sifu Po would have been so proud of me, if he'd known.

Chapter 25

"NORBIE FUCKING REINGRUBER," The Screw gloated, grinning a belt of gold-capped teeth, "Hamilton's number one retarded adolescent, the pasty fucking man-boy with the giant head, the Peter Pan fuck up, Humpty Dumpy YouTube star, and just for shits and giggles, the Village Vigilante on high fucking nerd alert."

We were in a cheap motel room that stank of factory sulphur and cigarette smoke. Stained beige drapes blocked the window. The cheap wood panelling had more than a few gross mystery stains, too.

I sat on a queen-size bed that looked like a rhino had used it as a trampoline, pressing my back against the headboard so I could keep an eye on everyone.

There was only one motel this close to Dofasco, so I was pretty sure I was being held hostage at the Lakeshore Motel. It was a motel my uncle Otto, a master bricklayer, had helped build back in the Fifties. No doubt he'd be saddened to see the state of his hard work all these years later: the peeling paint, the lurid red trim, and the sorry state of the people who patronized the motel.

One guy guarded the door, while the other two sat on the corners of the bed like sullen, overfed apes. Hunched over a small desk, sat a strange man dressed in black. He was fiddling with something.

"And who are you today?" The Screw asked, standing on the bed and trying to loom over me. "Kung Fu Norbie?" He barked laughter. "Are you going to kick the shit out of us and make a daring escape, just like one of your stupid superheroes in your little comic book? Isn't that how this superhero shit works? Huh, *nerd*?" He barked out another laugh. His thugs tightened their grips on their guns, just like the bad guys did in those film noir movies. What a cliché they were.

Rage stirred inside me. Only Donny had ever made me this mad. I held back, sensing this wasn't the right time to unleash it and fight for my life. The Screw's face still transfixed and disturbed me, as much as it had the first time I'd seen him at ComWorld. I was shocked, once again, at the way half his face sagged, how deeply its waxy folds hoarded shadow, and how its one, cold, egg white eye scanned its surroundings as if controlled by a second, sicker brain.

The Screw was clearly enjoying bullying me. And he obviously wanted to make sure I knew exactly how he felt about me.

"You're a pimple-faced lemming, *Eggie*, you know that, right? You went to high school, then took some dumb college level program to please your parents. How fucking predictable."

I squeezed my fists harder. *I'll show you who's predicable, Screw, just you wait!*

It would have been amazing if the Rainbow Army and the neo-Nazi skinheads would show up and go at it in the parking lot. All I needed was a split-second distraction so I could escape. Where was the cavalry when I needed them?

You're not in the Village any more, Norbie. There's no one here to save you. You have to save yourself.

The strange man fiddling at the desk turned and stood. Slowly, he approached me. His thin lips were so thin he barely had any.

Geez, he was creepy. He looked *exactly* like the ruthless Nazi Gestapo agent from *Raiders of the Lost Ark*. He had beady dark eyes, and his tiny hands gripped a scalpel and sharp scissors.

"This is Justin," The Screw said.

Justin? Seriously?

"So here's how it's going to go, Norbie. We ask you questions. Lie once and Justin cuts off a finger. Lie twice and he cuts off all your fingers. Lie three times, he cuts off your balls. Cry for help, and he cuts off your fucking head!"

Terrified, I involuntarily jerked off the bed. Two thugs shoved me back down and manacled my arms with mitts the size of steam shovels.

"So," The Screw began, inching his face close to mine, his googly eye drilling me with a funky death stare. "Who informed you that Shadow invented the Invisiblator?"

Justin clicked his scissors. *Snick snick!* They glinted under the overhead fluorescent light.

I was thinking of the perfect lie, one that sounded so true that even The Screw would believe it. *W.W.D.S: What Would Donny Say?* He was the ultimate liar.

"An *Invisiblator*," I said, dumbly. "What *Invisiblator*?"

The Screw's face curdled.

Think, idiot! Why is Donny such a good liar? The little boy inside me wanted to bawl. Tears flooded my eyes. I struggled against their grip, but the thugs were stupidly powerful, so I gave up. *Think, Norb. Why are Donny's lies so powerful? Well, because he believes them, that's why.*

The Screw nodded at Justin who inched his glinty scissors towards my upheld hand. Was I going to be maimed by a guy named *Justin*?

I guessed it didn't matter now, that I finally understood Donny's superpowers: believe your own lies. It wasn't going to save *me*.

The scissors kaleidoscoped in my eyes.

I felt sick to my stomach and wondered if I'd pass out. I hoped I would.

Then, by the grace of God, there was a powerful, intervening knock at the door.

Justin froze.

The three thugs drew their guns. One flattened his back against the wall beside the door and aimed his gun at chest level. Justin slipped his tools into an inside pocket of his tweed jacket. He looked quite sad.

"Who the fuck's there?" The Screw barked.

"Pizza and wings for Eldon Cratchley," the delivery guy said. He sounded like a teenager.

"No one here by that name," The Screw said. He cleared his throat, looking slightly sheepish. "There must be some mistake."

"Paid for by a Mr. Shadow?" the delivery kid said. "Three extra-large pizzas, double cheese, pepperoni, and hot peppers. Plus sixty hot wings. Real fat and juicy, too, best wings in the Hammer, dude."

Eldon Cratchley? I thought. *Is that The Screw's real name? Holy cow!* <u>*Way*</u> *nerdier than mine!*

Everyone was licking their chops. So was I, despite knowing my fingers were on the chopping block.

The Screw zipped over to the door. "This better be legit, asshole, or you'll wish you never met me." He gave me a hard look.

Yeah, I get it. No funny business. I sat up straight and tried to look happy to be there.

He jammed his gun into his belt and whipped open the door.

Standing there was a red-headed teen boy with a goofy smile, holding three pizza boxes and a big bag of wings and wearing of all things a red *Making Steven Famous* ball cap. Then it dawned on me. Morag! Her disguise was totally believable. *What nerve! What courage!*

My heart was pounding, I was that worried for her. What on earth was she planning? If it didn't work, she was done for!

As a thug swiped the food out of her arms, Morag said, "Mr. Shadow asked us to make them extra special, so we put a surprise in every box, just like he asked." She gave the dwarf a dopey smile. "He said he really is proud of you fellas. And he was real nice on the phone when he placed his order."

The Screw's face suddenly crinkled with suspicion. "A surprise in every box, huh? Is this a fucking joke?"

The muscle men tensed.

One of the men plopped the food down on a wobbly formica table beneath the window. He pointed his gun at the boxes, and eyed them suspiciously, as if expecting something inside to leap out and attack him. His lips parted, his eyes glassed over—the heavenly aroma of pizza was getting to him.

Even my mouth watered.

The Screw gave one long lick of his greasy chops. He nodded at his goon.

The guy flipped open the pizza boxes.

"What the fuck?" he said, as a puff of steam hit his face. He blinked.

Three pepperoni pizzas. *Mmmm.*

For a split second, everything looked normal.

The Screw was about to shut the door on Morag but something changed his mind. His googly eye went from stupid sleepy to royally pissed.

I saw what he saw.

Under the box lids, someone had drawn goofy images of the Screw and his thugs engaged in indecent sexual acts. With each other! Right away I recognized Morag's work. She was an excellent artist when she wanted to be, or in this case *needed* to be. *Morag, what on God's green earth were you thinking?*

Eyes wide, Morag flipped the Screw the bird and high-tailed it.

"Run, honey!" I shrieked, proud and terrified.

The Screw motioned to two of his men to chase Morag and they did, The Screw scurrying out behind them. That left just one guy and Justin to guard me.

Had that been her plan? To give me a few precious seconds to escape?

Determined to be Morag's real-life superhero, not some bogus made-up one like the Steeltown Avenger, I leapt off the bed up onto the table, upending pizza onto the floor. I ripped open the drapes, covered my face with my hands so I wouldn't shred my eyes, and dove through the window like Super Norbie, shattering glass everywhere, belly-flopping on the strip of dirty sidewalk. The impact knocked the wind out of me.

The remaining thug ran out of the Motel, hovered over me, and pointed his gun at my face. "Don't move, idiot." He surveyed the dimly lit parking lot for trouble, saw none, then stared back down at me. "What a dumb move. You shredded yourself, man."

I could feel blood on my head and forearms. My entire body felt battered. I lay still, praying for my breath to return, choking down on the urge to cry. A gust of wind scuffed an empty Humpty Dumpty chip bag along the parking lot and up against my leg. *Wow. Thanks, universe.*

It occurred to me that I probably should have just run out the door.

There was no sign of Morag. I pictured The Screw going to all the trouble of joining in the chase for my wife. Thank God she could run like the wind!

Justin scurried out the front door, slipped into his Austin Mini, and raced away. Maybe he was late for another torture appointment.

In the near distance, there were gunshots. For a moment, everything went fuzzy. Morag is *not* dead. Morag is *not* dead, I told myself, like a little prayer.

There were three cars parked in the lot. A prostitute and her John hurried into a black BMW and sped off over the potholed asphalt, spooked by the gunfire.

I was certain the only reason I wasn't dead yet had everything to do with The Screw. He could easily have killed me by now. He definitely wanted to. Somehow, he must need me. What for? No doubt it all came down to the Invisiblator—an imaginary device, for crying out loud!

All at once, a spray of bullets pinged the motel wall, blasting out chunks of brick. The thug keeled over with a shriek, clutching his leg.

"Holy cow!" I shouted, watching his leg spurt blood.

His gun had skittered along the sidewalk. Slowly, he crawled towards it. I painfully hauled myself up and was about to beat him to it.

A Ford Tempo with a mismatched hood screeched towards us.

"Right, Norbie!" a familiar voice cried. "Let's go, soldier!" To the goon, he said, "Just lie there, nice and still, unless you want a bullet in yer heed."

It was Archie Love! And he'd brought the cavalry! Tony, Donny, and John whipped out of the car and raced towards me. Poking through the back window was a smoking machine gun barrel. On the other end of it was Mr. Love, grinning like the Joker. For once, I was really happy to see him.

My buds were half-way to me when two black sedans screeched to a halt in front of them. Out flew official-looking men in suits, guns pointed at all of us. "Stop right there! Federal officers!"

Everyone froze.

Slowly, grumbling something nasty and incoherent, even Mr. Love dropped his hands from his machine gun and reluctantly did as he was told.

Some I.D. was flashed in our faces. I caught a familiar name from one of the badges.

Were these the same agents Donny had told us about, I wondered. Smith and Smith, the agents from CSIS? The ones that had interrogated Donny above the pot shop to see if Steven really was alive? Did this mean that the agents in the second car were the American agents Donny had also told us about? *Am I fuzzing dreaming, or what?*

One of the feds gazelled over and stomped on the thug's arm a split second before he got a chance to raise his gun off the ground. Then I looked up to see his partner lean over me, preparing to jab a needle into my arm. Both agents had a very satisfied look.

And that was the last thing I remembered.

Chapter 26

A HOMELESS-LOOKING man, fresh off the cover of Jethro Tull's Aqualung album, dropped a quarter into my empty Tim Horton's coffee cup. His eyes were badly bloodshot, his breath way worse than Mr. Love's. "Hang in there, brother."

I stared at him blankly.

"Thanks," I mumbled. *What a nice guy.*

I couldn't remember drinking the coffee, or ordering it. I was lying on the concrete, my back up against the brick wall. *What am I doing here?*

I watched the man push his rusted shopping cart and its cargo of beer cans and wine bottles along the narrow sidewalk in front of Tim Hortons. I shielded my eyes against the blazing sun. It hurt my eyes and made my head hurt.

I checked my watch. Nine-thirty in the morning. *What am I doing sitting outside the coffee shop near my apartment? Why do I feel so out of it?*

A few metres away, some bikers hung out and chatted. I squinted at them. It was the same guys who'd been ready to pound me when they thought I'd hurt Morag. Between sips of coffee, a few of them nodded at me sympathetically. "Had a rough night, bud?" one asked.

Had I? I sagged, trying to remember the night before. My *gi* top was back on, but hanging open.

I slowly dragged myself into a sitting position. I felt like a wet sack of cement. My head was numb, my mouth totally parched. My lips felt fat and weird.

Determined to make sure my loved ones were safe, I fumbled for my phone in my pocket and, after five failed attempts, finally got Morag's number right.

"Norb, oh my gawd, are you okay? Did those guys hurt you?"

"No, no' really, thort of." My tongue wouldn't cooperate.

"What? Did they hit you in the head? What did they *do* to you? Norbie?"

The world was spinning so hard I had to shut my eyes to keep from barfing. Somehow, I forced the words out of my mush-mouth. "The feds thowed up and drugged me with thome kind of truth therum, I think. I can't feel my legth."

"Wait just a minute," said Morag. "Is this The Screw, *pretending* to be my husband? If it is, I swear I'll put a bullet in your fucking head, you little bastard!"

"Ith me," I managed. "Nor."

"Prove it. What was the name of my childhood dog?"

I thought about that for a moment. "Anguth, or wath it Goldie?"

She sighed with relief. "Jesus, Norb, Goldie was the name of my goldfish, but close enough. Where are you?"

"Tim'th, on Th-teel Th-treet."

"Good, there's lots of witnesses, so it's unlikely The Screw will try anything."

"Are you th-till at the Tartan Club?" I asked.

"No, we ran as soon as The Screw kidnapped you. We booked two adjoining rooms down at the Royal Connaught Hotel, under an alias. The Dads brought their machine guns, so we should be okay, unless the crazy bastards have another WWII argument and shoot each other."

"*Gee whith,*" I said. "The dadth are bumhead crathy. At leatht everyone'th thafe for now. Promith me you won't go anywhere until I finith off the dwarf."

"Finish off that little a-hole? Not by yourself! That's way too dangerous. I'll be there in fifteen minutes, Norb! Don't go anywhere!"

"No! Morag, don't! I have a plan, and it involvth you."

"A plan?"

"I'll call you later today and tell you, I promith."

"I'm not taking *no* for—"

"I have to call Karl and make thure Mutti is thafe. I love you, Morag!" I hastily hung up.

It hurt to hang up on Morag—I felt like a real piece of *sheet*.

I dialed Karl. I made a concerted effort to master my thick tongue.

"Norbie! Is everything okay? I talked to Morag last night."

"Everyone's okay, Karl."

"You sound stoned, Norb. Did the feds drug you with truth serum? I hear they do that from time to time."

"They do, but I'm okay. How's Mutti?"

"Fear not," he said with his best Dracula voice. "Norman and I are on the case. No sign of The Screw or his evil thugs. But if he does show, Karl the Great will have a big surprise for him." Even when Karl was trying to be sincere, he sounded like he was putting on a show.

"Do you want to talk to her?"

"Not now, Karl. Please tell her I love her. I'll be over as soon as I can."

As I hung up, a mother and her daughter stepped over my outstretched leg. "Sorry, ma'am." I drew it into me. The little girl asked her mom what was wrong with me. Her mom shushed her and hurried her along.

My cheeks burned with embarrassment at being all beefed-out on the ground, in public, in broad daylight. But no matter how hard I tried, I couldn't stand up. Exhaustion had throttled the crap out my muscles.

The drive-thru line-up was so long it snaked out into the main parking lot. Through their car windows, a few people stared at me, some with real disgust. Two black pick-up trucks with roofing decals on their doors inched past, but those guys paid me no notice. It was Hamilton, after all, and in some parts of the city, a guy passed out in public was as normal as the stink of factory smokestacks.

The sudden memory of the night before adrenalized me and launched me up onto my feet. I fought the terrible dizziness trying to spin me back down onto the sidewalk. It felt like the time I rode the Salt and Pepper shaker at the Canadian National Exhibition.

"Hey, look who's awake," a biker said. "It's the Village Vigilante, fighting crime, one donut at a time."

There was scattered laughter, but it wasn't mean.

"Hey, sorry to see that your mom's house got burned, man. Hope they catch the fucker that did that." There was agreement the arsonist deserved a beat-down.

I think I smiled at them.

My heart was doing double time, and I swayed dangerously, but I kept my feet.

I remembered how, last year, CSIS had interrogated Donny in a room above a pot shop, and had pressured him to spill the beans on his relationship to Steven Dundee. Donny had cooked up crazy stories about Steven in his bogus *In Town* columns. He'd inadvertently risked national security with his lies, and they were pissed. Donny had said CSIS had tried to bribe him with donuts. And, then, they'd drugged him with truth serum, giving him a wicked case of Jimmy legs.

Had they drugged me? Why? Over The Screw? Over Mr. Love and his fuzzin' arsenal from Hell?

Go piss up Donny's tree, I thought, *not mine*.

But the more I thought about it, the more certain I was that CSIS' interest in me had everything to do with The Screw, Shadow and the Invisiblator. If I'd known, when I created the Steeltown Avenger, that all hell would break loose, would I have continued? I don't know. Ask Dr. Tom Collins. It's really all *his* fault. He took on a life of his own. I just drew him and wrote him. He's the one who wanted to do more than just be a nuclear medicine specialist at McMaster Hospital. He wanted to fight crime. He wanted to don his grey and black armour with the red A over the heart and become the Steeltown Avenger. He's the one who invented the Invisiblator, which allowed him sixty seconds of invisibility, giving him an edge over the scum of the underworld.

Had I somehow made the Invisiblator possible, simply by imagining it?

No no no. You don't make things real by thinking them! Otherwise, I would have a pet Ewok by now. Still, the possibility of Shadow rendering evil guys invisible really frightened me. The implications were staggering, and I didn't want to think about any of that anymore, so I shut it down.

I experienced a single, foggy memory. I remember being crashed out in the back of the CSIS sedan, as the hazy light of dawn pressed against the rear window. They were at the Tim Horton's drive-thru. They bought me a coffee, then got out of the car and dumped me in front. They could have dumped me behind a bush so people wouldn't see me, but that's when I realized, without a doubt, that CSIS agents could be cruel and unethical.

I grabbed my phone out of my pocket. At least, they'd left me that.

My voicemail box was full. I didn't care.

The pot of creativity and fear that had been cooking away on the back burner of my mind for days now boiled over. Ideas fused, fresh colourful ink on a story board. With a mind of their own, my fingers punched in a phone number. With stunning clarity, I knew exactly what had to be done, who would do it, and why.

Now only half-dizzied from drugs, I staggered along Steel Street towards Mutti's house, barking orders into my phone like a raging Hitler.

Chapter 27

MORAG LOVED TWILIGHT. She always said it was a magical time.

So that's why I'd picked twilight to kick The Screw's ass.

Hey, Screw! Watch me pull a rabbit out of my hat, you fuzzin' arch-hole!

Donny had gotten really excited over the role I assigned him. At first, Tony and John pushed back, but neither could think of a better plan, so eventually they caved. The Showdown of Showdowns would begin smack-dab in the middle of twilight, at eight forty-five sharp.

Dad's Luger was cool and smooth in my hands as I surveyed Mutti's burnt-out garage. As a kid, Dad had driven me to the Hamilton Gun Club and shown me how to fire it. I'd always been a little nervous around guns, but after yesterday's insane Tarantino shoot-out at the Tartan Club, I totally wasn't.

I loaded the magazine clip and clicked it into the gun. I was surprised how easily I did that. Like riding a bike. I slid it into my shoulder holster. Mutti couldn't stand that Dad had owned a gun, and she'd badgered him to get rid of it, but he'd said it was good to have in case of an emergency. He'd believed Nazis were everywhere, hiding in plain sight, even in Canada, waiting for the right moment to rise up again. We thought he was paranoid. Mutti had said he was paranoid, but it turned out he'd worried for good reason, considering the events of the past few days.

I thought of the neo-Nazis clashing with the Rainbow warriors outside my shop, and realized just how right my dad had been. And, on top of that, there was an evil dwarf and his criminal mastermind boss. And Justin-the-Torturer. Who knew how many other wicked forces were at play in the world? Maybe cosplayers weren't as whacked-out as everyone liked to think. Maybe the world was more like animé than we knew.

I tucked five magazine clips into my utility belt which fit perfectly around my waist. Beneath my grey cape, the Luger was barely visible.

The garage reeked of smoke. My Atari 7800 video game console had melted like a Salvador Dali sculpture. *Can't hold onto your past forever, Norb.*

Shut up! I know that already! Geez!

Everything else was charred beyond recognition. There was a massive hole in the roof.

I was grateful the fire hadn't penetrated the house, but the yard was a shambles. The ground was soggy and full of charred wood. Candy wrappers, empty chip bags, and crushed pop cans littered the lawn. The so-called fans had done nothing to help me in my time of need. And why did they see me as a hero? I hadn't done anything to help them, either. Well, not yet.

I yanked The Screw's business card out of my utility belt and dialed.

The Screw was steaming. "Norbie, you fu—"

"Shut your fuzzin' pie hole and listen to me!" Then I shouted orders and immediately hung up, so I wouldn't have to hear his stupid backtalk.

I checked my watch. It was go-time.

"Let's rock!"

And there I was, the Steeltown Avenger, wearing my trademark grey cape. I had the body armour, the boots, the mask, the scarlet A shining proudly over my heart. Dr. Tom Collins would have been so proud, man. And I was going to kick The Screw's arse.

I sprinted, knowing exactly where I'd end up after I gassed out, and exactly what I'd do to foil that piece of shit dwarf.

Chapter 28

IRONICALLY, I GASSED out next to the gas station on the southwest corner of the Village. A strong wind flapped my cape as I hunched over, wheezing.

I resisted the powerful temptation to nip over to Mike's for a sub. This was progress. *Good for you, Norb.* I pried my gaze from the sub shop and focussed on the real task at hand.

Traffic was heavy. I swear that Donny's billboard had developed an attitude. The orangey footlights garishly shone on the bizarre image of our old high school classmate Dave Walker, who for all we knew was dead. Of course, I'd thought that about Steven at one time, too. Dave was dressed like Willy Wonka, standing with his back to the viewer, his legs crossed at the ankles, his right hand behind his back with its fingers crossed. What a cheesy Loverboy rip-off. What *was* cool was that Dave jutted out from the billboard a bit, in 3D. Beside the fake Dave, was the cover of Donny's novel, which was actually quite impressive. In bold letters was Donny's pseudonym, Dave Walker. *Worst name for a pseudonym! Boring!* I thought. Even worse because he'd ripped off a real guy's name! If Walker was alive, he'd totally freak, hire a lawyer and sue Donny's ass, or maybe just strangle him to death. Personally, I liked both options.

Donny's billboard looked like it was about to come to life. Given recent events, it wouldn't surprise me. But the way I was feeling, if a giant Willy Wonka Dave Walker started walking the streets, I was the Oompa Loompa who would take him down.

When I'd called and told Morag my plan, she'd said I'd lost my mind and that my plan was bumhead insane. Despite all that, she admitted there was half a chance it might work, but only with an absurd amount of luck. She'd demanded she be given a role in the takedown, and wasn't taking no for an answer. Of course, I told her I'd already cooked a role up for her, a juicy one, which would make her happy, but she wasn't getting the details until she got here. And only if she came with Tank, so she'd be safer that way. To be honest, I'd only said that so I'd have time to come up with something. Sometimes we procrastinators get the best ideas under pressure. Oh well. I was a work in progress.

Some people thought I sounded like I'd taken too many hits to the head. But things aren't always as they seem. Ask Karl the Great. My brain actually had a brain. My revenge plan had poofed into my mind fully-formed. Although my plan wasn't completely grounded in reality, I was pretty sure that wouldn't get in the way of its brilliant success.

I ran across the crosswalk, energized by the twilight sky. Morag was right. It was a magical time. My red A felt almost tingly on my chest.

I found myself stopping in front of the The Blue Ball. Its large window threw back my reflection.

Thanks to the fast and professional work of Incognito Master Patricia and her crack team on Kingslea Drive, my suit was amazing. Two hours earlier I'd stopped in and they'd fashioned me into the hero I was destined to be, the same Steeltown Avenger I'd imagined when Dr. Tom Collins first burst into my imagination. The crimson A gleamed over my heart. The grey body armour, edged in black, the mask, the steel-toed boots, the utility belt packed with everything a crime-fighter could need was all awesome. *I* was awesome.

I saw a motherly women walk past the bait, as I'd come to think of it. When she saw it, her face froze in shock, and she dropped her bowling ball bag. She quickly picked it up and scurried into the bowling alley.

Seeing it for the first time, plucked out of my imagination and made perfectly real, a wave of queasy heat flushed my body. The quicker this was over the better.

I couldn't believe I'd found a way to get the thing built.

Donny had come through. Donny always knew a guy, but for once he'd definitely found the right guy for this job.

It felt weird to see the shop fired up on a Monday night. The lights were normally out by six. But tonight, nothing was normal.

The Screw had had me hopping around like a Mexican jumping bean for days, with his fuzzin' deadlines and ultimatums. Well, now *I* was giving the orders.

We'd see who was jumping for whom.

"Nice costume, fatty," a teen laughed, passing a joint to his friends inside a nearby bus shelter. They were high as kites. I ran over and slapped him in the melon. "Respect your elders," I growled. "And no smoking in city bus shelters! Can't you read the sign?" Then I coughed a little, because I'm just not built to do a growl.

"Hey, man, what the fuck?" he said, rubbing his sore cheek. "Did you guys see that?"

I sprinted away from him past Tim Hortons, towards the back of the bowling alley and the ladder I'd planted there earlier that day. I was going to meet a guy there, a guy Donny knew, a guy who knew a guy. I had to pay him to do a job.

Behind me, in the distance, I heard the other teens laughing at their friend. I was glad I'd put that kid in his place. Maybe I was the Village Vigilante after all. *Or maybe you're the fuzzin' Steeltown Avenger, more like it!* And maybe I'd always been super-capable but hadn't recognized that in myself. Wearing the costume definitely made me feel powerful and fearless. *I should have suited up years ago.*

A young couple standing outside of Hortons eyed me suspiciously, but that was totally understandable. It's not often you spot a real superhero in your midst, his cape flapping in the breeze. Their little dog yipped at me, straining on its leash.

After my errand, I ran through the back entrance of the bowling alley, then sprinted the entire length, serenaded by the sound of whirring balls and crashing pins.

The place was packed with league bowlers. At the far end, there was a snack bar with a sweeping green formica countertop. I rushed past it, and stopped at the front doors, crouching down behind a planter full of plastic flowers. The league bowlers coming in and out gave me looks of shock and disgust.

Each time the door swung open, I got a blast of cool air, which felt really good against my sweaty skin. I hoped no one called the police on me. If they only knew that I had lives to save, they'd surely have left me alone to do my job, and some might even have offered to help me.

Right on schedule, The Screw's car screeched up the curb and then disappeared from sight as he wheeled to the west end of the parking lot.

From behind the planter, I watched as he and his crew came back to the front of the building on foot, scanning uneasily for witnesses.

As they shambled past the door towards my shop, I saw them discreetly draw their guns. I prayed my plan didn't backfire. I had to admit, that up until now, I'd been totally psyched to see the look of horror and rage on that creep's face when he actually saw the *bait*. But now I wasn't so sure I wanted to see him *that* angry.

The Screw suddenly stopped. His men eyed him nervously.

He was so royally pissed I thought his googly eye was going to twang out of its socket and blow a hole through a passing bus! His jaw unhinged like an ancient steam shovel.

Even through the glass door, I could hear him cursing in a language I didn't recognize. They probably only spoke it in Middle Earth. He stared, vibrating, caught in some kind of foggy mental dilemma.

My plan was going beautifully. So, of course, something was probably about to go wrong.

I eased the door open and slid along to a small brick outcrop in the wall between the bowling alley and my shop. I peered out from behind it and watched. I couldn't breathe. My heart was bumping in my ears.

In front of the shop, on a steel pedestal, sat the bait. It was a *papier maché* replica of my Invisiblator. I'd paid Donny's guy to build it to my exact specifications. It stood ten feet tall.

The Screw's rage had been my goal. The high-tech Invisiblator had been modified to look like a massive, half-erect, robot cock. Dangling from its tip hung a life-size effigy of my enemy, his lips firmly wrapped around the tip. A strong breeze was swinging the effigy back and forth. The Screw was literally a dangling cocksucker.

A little gaggle of elderly bowlers had stopped on their way to their cars and pointed at the eyesore. "What the hell *is* that?" an old bird said, squinting in confusion. Her husband figured it was a promotional stunt. "Maybe there's a new comic book coming out." The woman said, "Oh, I know who runs that place. The Village Vigilante, or bloody Humpty Dumpty, or whatever that fool calls himself these days." She scoffed. "What's this city coming to?" Still, despite her disgust, she couldn't pry her eyes away from the masterpiece. I wondered if the *The Steeltown Avenger* comics might appeal to a wider market than Tye had anticipated.

The two ladies with them tittered. They had a very different take on what they were seeing.

The bowlers were so taken with the phallus and its dangler, they hadn't noticed the menacing criminals scowling at them. Invisiblator sex had clearly blinded the bowlers to the reality of evil in their midst! *Unbelievable!*

Across the road, doing the worst job of hiding behind a Canada Post box, was John. There was a gleam of light off his shiny shoes. Beneath the box, something glittered like broken glass. I sighed with relief. The sarcastic bumhead was exactly where I'd told him to be at exactly the right time. For once, he'd actually listened to me.

Further up the sidewalk, three teenage girls had stopped and were pointing at the Invisiblator, falling into each other's arms with screeches of laughter.

The Screw found his resolve and skittered towards the door of my shop like a desperate rat, his huge shoes slapping the tarmac. His thugs stayed close, turning and scanning the Village.

Satisfied that things were rolling out as planned, I high-tailed it.

Chapter 29

I FELT TERRIBLY DIZZY, not from sprinting the length of the alley, or zipping up the ladder out back, or running across the rooftop to meet my guy, but from teetering on the roof edge above my apartment. The little buzz-tard would see me when the time was exactly right. A strong wind flapped my cape. I felt like the maestro of the Village. All I needed was a conductor's baton. Or better yet, an Invisiblator.

The bowling alley sign pulsed red and blue light in the night, making me pulse, too, a magic version of the Steeltown Avenger.

The crack of gunfire from below startled me, although I'd expected it. I nearly lost my balance. *Stay alert, Norb!*

I ran my fingers along the cold steel of Dad's Luger, trying to reassure myself that everything would work out.

The Screw and his men had blustered into my shop and plugged bullets into our effigies, courtesy of Patricia and her Incognito team, either because they'd thought they were real, or out of sheer rage when they realized they'd been set up, again!

Thanks to Donny's technical savvy, all this thuggery was being caught on video. He'd installed a tiny camera in the display case behind my Thor action figure.

I knew The Screw would be out of his mind with rage and frustration. But, again, that's how I'd planned it. I'd finally realized that if I could plot and write a fantasy crime story for a comic book, I sure as heck could devise a *real* plan and carry it out in *real* life, or at least die trying.

I kept balling and re-balling my courage against the dizzying height up there on the roof. I wasn't sure how much longer I could stay upright.

I watched John run-skate-dance across Flux Road, just like he raced up the wing during road hockey. He charged up and over the sidewalk, skated the narrow band of tarmac, whipped open the shop door and tossed in a tear gas canister, courtesy of the Tartan Club munitions depot. The metal made a *tinking* sound as it struck the tiled floor. John high-tailed it.

I heard the men inside shouting.

They stumbled out of my shop, hacking violently.

And that's when Donny started barking nonsense into a megaphone, also as ordered by yours truly. He'd always been a master of nonsense, and a master of fuzzing up people's lives, including his own, and now, finally, he was able to put his skills to good use. His talents were mostly of the Devil, and I'd had to console myself with the knowledge that Donny was usually intent on doing the right thing despite old Lucifer pulling most of the levers in his brain.

He was pacing back and forth on the narrow catwalk beneath his billboard, the flood lights casting his shadow way up. He was the Jim Carrey of carnival barkers.

"Hey Screw! Nice eye, brother! Ever thought of donating it to science? Or maybe feed it to your boyfriends. They look a little undernourished, don't you think?" He wheezed a crazed laugh. Then he went onto a predictably self-indulgent tangent. "Weesty beesty hi-ho heesty!" Then he sang, "Hi Ho, Hi Ho, It's Off To Work We Go":

"The Screw, The Screw,
So much to do,
To show the world he's better than you,
His size of shoe is overwrought,
Twice the size of his store-bought cock!
Bwaahhhh!"

And it just went downhill from there.

But I had to give it to Donny—he was really getting under The Screw's skin. And he'd actually followed through on my instructions. *Unbelievable!*

"Get him!" The Screw screamed, pointing up at the billboard. He'd forgotten about all the civilians witnessing this sheet-show.

One of the guys made a beeline for lunatic Donny. How he thought he'd actually get up there, I had no idea.

I turned and nodded at my guy on the roof.

"Hey, Screw!" I shouted down to him.

My guy tipped a huge kettle of roofing tar. The Screw caught the movement of the flow heading straight at him, but bolted too late. It swashed his leg, the impact collapsing him against the ground, where he began thrashing, trying to paw away the hot tar that had melted through his pants and was burning and bubbling his flesh. He screamed like a wounded, enraged animal.

Another thug escaped the hot torrent but his associate wasn't as lucky. It splashed the back of his neck and knocked him to the ground. He was wailing.

The scalding goo spread along the tarmac. I waved off my guy, so he righted the kettle.

I hadn't wanted to kill The Screw, only stop him in his tracks until the police showed up. I really hoped someone had called them by now. In case no one had, I thought I'd better. I was about to dial 911 when the unscathed thug looked skyward and fired his gun at me.

I caught the play in the nick of time. I jerked back from the edge as the bullet whizzed past my ear. Across the street, John skated to safety behind the mailbox just as a bullet pinged the metal.

Now was my chance for the final stage of my plan. After that, I had absolutely nothing. The rest was up to everybody else. I'd told all my friends to improvise using their God-given talents. I'd felt pretty confident Tony and John would do just that, and Donny was doing a bang-up job, ranting away across the street.

I ran along the rooftop edge, grabbed the coil of rope I'd attached to a bolt at the top of the bowling alley sign, and inhaled super deeply. Then I jumped, swinging through the air past the pulsing neon lights, shouting at the top of my lungs. Originally, my plan had been to shout: "the Steeltown Avenger, destroying evil, one Screw at a time!" I think what came out was sort of more of a wordless yodel. But the spirit was still fairly heroic, even though my bowels quivered.

I'd also planned to swing past the sign, and on the way back slide down the rope, land on the ground, and battle The Screw, but in mid-swing, my cape snagged on the sign's letter B, the sudden jerk popping my Luger out of my belt. It spiraled downward through the air, hit the ground, and fired a random shot. *Fuzz!*

I was now dangling above The Screw, unarmed.

He grabbed my Dad's Luger and pointed it at me, and sneered, staggering on his burned leg. "Say goodbye, Norbie, you piece-of-shit nerd!"

"Care for a Glasgow kiss, ya ugly goblin?"

The Screw spun around, stupified.

And that's when Jimmy head-butted his face, cracking it like an egg. Blood spurted out his nostrils. The gun flew out of The Screw's hands, clattering against the ground.

"Welcome to *Glasgee*!" Jimmy cried.

Then he looked down and realized he was flying low. Calmly, he zipped up his pants. Through a crack in the barber shop drapes, I could just make out a shapely pair of legs. Jimmy was entertaining a lady-friend after-hours, something that happened a lot more often than you'd expect.

The Screw was doubled over, his face in hands, whimpering, blood running between his fingers. The guy on the ground was still clutching his burned neck.

But the other thug was just about to fire at me when he froze.

"*Shazaammy-zam-zam!*" It was Karl! He was crouched in the parking lot, and launched a bowling ball along the pavement toward The Screw. Except that it wasn't a bowling ball. It looked like something Wile E. Coyote would use. It even had a wick, sizzling as it burned. We all just stared, mesmerized.

Jimmy had lit up a filterless smoke at some point, and now he calmly backed away from the area of impending impact.

The bomb rolled to a gentle stop against The Screw's huge shoe. Perfectly bowled! He flinched, blood dripping off his chin. You could see the wheels turning. Was this a gag?

Yes, and no.

The bomb exploded with a long, loud fart, like the world's best whoopie cushion, spewing out rainbow smoke filled with glitter. At that moment, the neon "B" gave way under my weight. Metal screeched as I began to sink toward the ground, my cape ripping. All at once, I dropped the final ten feet, down through the sparkling cloud. I felt myself land on someone, cushioned from injury. There was a sudden crack of gun fire.

Through the smoke chaos came the nasty sound of squealing tires and a heaving engine: roaring, squealing, roaring, heaving, over and over.

A gust of wind cleared the sparkling smoke.

On the hood of his painstakingly rebuilt Camaro, in bold red letters, Tony had painted "Italian Stallion". Yellow and orange flames were painted along the sides. A gleaming vent-thing jutted out of the engine. His car was totally bad-ass. Now the Tone-Mobile was pinning the only remaining henchman to the wall of the plaza. Carefully, of course. Tony Valentini has always been meticulous.

The pinned thug looked stony, a no-good welcoming certain death. His gun was out of reach on the hood. Tony's expression, on the other hand, was very familiar: a tightly wound coil of molten wire. Man, he was pissed off!

I was about to congratulate him, when I was shoved upward. An angry little goblin rolled out from underneath me and chased after Karl.

"Gimme my fuckin' gun, you freak!"

Karl was grinning, dancing away from us like Stevie Nicks on steroids, holding the Screw's gun and Dad's Luger just up out of reach. The Screw jumped up and down like a frustrated little kid, screeching with frustration.

"Argh!" The Screw cried.

But Karl twirled away like a fast-spinning top. He was incredibly nimble for a senior citizen.

Next thing I knew, Morag and Tank had un-corked out of a cab, and were battling the burned thug who was trying to make a Hail Mary. Turns out I didn't have to give Morag a role. She knew exactly what to do!

The Screw had given up chasing Karl for his gun and turned back toward me, infuriated. He swung his fist at me. It was the size of a small wrecking ball.

Reflexively, and oh how I'd planned to do this when the time was just right, I dropped to the ground in a full-on splits. It was going to be an epic Steeltown Avenger moment.

But all the times I'd practiced at home, I hadn't been wearing body armour or a utility belt. At the last second, I tightened up. Uh oh.

The pain was excruciating, as if someone had driven thousands of hot needles into my groin.

"*Fuuuuuccckkkkk!!!!!!!!!!!!!!!!*"

Somehow, I rolled away before that creep landed on top of me.

I was half-way to my feet when The Screw drove the tip of his pointy shoe under my kneecap, an exploding pain crumpling me to the ground. Then he mounted my chest and started boxing my face. It happened so fast. I was stunned at the oddity of it all.

It would have been a great moment for some police cars to show up. Even a few neo-Nazis.

Almost automatically, I stopped his punches with outside circle blocks, but then I missed a real doozy and it smashed against the side of my head, good and proper. I felt as if I'd been pounded by a giant ham.

This time I really did vomit. All over my chest. The Screw didn't miss a beat and kept hammering away at me, vomit flicking and spraying everywhere.

Dimly, I noticed a pretty sparkle above my head. Was that a disco ball flying through the air? I heard the sound of glass smashing over toward the barbershop, John yelling "Sorry!" which made no sense. Once more, there was a sparkling overhead, a thud, and then the sound of Morag and Tank cheering. "Way to go, John!" Morag yelled. "That's one down!"

The Screw went to punch me again, but this time I hand-blocked his elbow, drove it into my center line, pinned it against my chest, locked my foot against the outside of his leg so he couldn't post, raised my hips and threw him off of me.

"Nicely done, Norbie," said a familiar voice.

I stumbled to my feet. "Sifu Po?" Had he really come all this way to help his old student? Had I really meant that much to him? I bowed, chunks of vomit falling to the pavement. I was very unsteady on my feet.

"Please, Norbie," he said, smiling, "allow me." And, just as The Screw popped up off the ground like the feisty bed bug he was, my old sifu lunged through the air at him with a skipping front kick, his silver hair flashing in the night air. He drove the heel of his shoe into the goblin's barrel chest. The impact drove The Screw skittering backwards through the glass of the bowling alley doors. He landed on his butt just past the lip of the door frame, stunned. His googly eye was dilating with fishy fear. How was this guy still alive, after all this abuse? Come to think of it, how was *I* still alive?

"Strike!" Mr. Po shouted.

Looky-loo bowlers who'd gathered at the doors had jerked back just in time to avoid being struck by the flying glass.

In the distance, there was a wail of sirens. *Finally!*

"Help!" Donny cried through the megaphone.

I'd forgotten about Donny! Across the intersection, he was dueling it out with the last of The Screw's men, who had somehow climbed up to the billboard catwalk. Their shadows danced. Were those swords? Long swords? *For fuzz sakes!* How long had they been fighting? It was one thing for a trained LARP-er to duel, but Donny was just an unskilled, normative citizen. When this was over, maybe he would like to try Live Action Role Play.

A gasp went up from the crowd. I needed to get up there, now!

From close by, Sifu Po said, "Your friends and I have things in hand. You should get up there, Norbie." He had clamped The Screw in a rear-naked choke hold.

I had one quick detour. I jogged around to the back of the bowling alley. By the time I came back to the front again, the little bonfire in the pretentious black muscle car was probably nicely taking hold. I'd used a ComWorld souvenir lighter. It seemed appropriate.

I raced toward the intersection, preparing to fight my way through the crowds to get across the street to Donny. But people ignored me, entertained by the flames that shot up into the night sky as The Screw's car burned.

Behind Aurora Pizzeria, at the foot of the billboard, I looked up. Donny was on his back. The thug was pounding his face and head. At least they weren't fighting with longswords anymore!

Donny was doing his best to rubber out from under the thug, but the guy's powerful thighs kept Donny pinned, and his blows struck more often than not. They bounced Donny's head off the catwalk like a super ball.

John had skated after me as I sprinted around back of the pizzeria. "Look at that, Norb!" he said.

We stared in awe at a vintage brown ACE motorcycle leaning against the tower. Then, I remembered Donny saying he'd planned to buy a motorcycle like Steven's. At the time, I'd put it down as another crazy notion. But, here it was, exactly how I would have envisioned it. Exactly!

The yelps coming from above us reminded me that Donny was being pummelled. I soared up the ladder like a real fuzzin' superhero. John was right on my heels. At the top, we discovered Donny's hockey stick jammed between the rungs; on the shaft, in black marker, *The Village Idiots*, and beside it, *Lannie*. Oh, so this was the longsword.

He had repaired this battered, beloved Lannie MacDonald hockey stick countless times, since he was twelve. There was only one to thing to do now. I looked at John and his eyes narrowed. *Yes.*

I yanked the stick out, poked my head above the ladder, and located the thug, wailing on Donny. Beside him, on the catwalk, was Donny's megaphone and a second hockey stick. Had he had actually given the thug a stick to fight with? Huh. Donny had always been about the fair fight. He probably would love LARP.

I slipped stealthily up onto the catwalk.

I took three measured steps, wound up with everything I had, and cried, "S.A. strikes again!"

The guy had barely turned around when I'd delivered the wickedest, most powerful Bobby Hull slap shot of my entire fuzzin' life! The blade smashed his face and knocked him off of Donny, rendering him unconscious before he slammed against the catwalk. Blood guzzled out of a nasty gash on his cheek. The impact sent one half of the stick boomeranging upward through the air. It hit the billboard, busting the Loverboy-esque crossed fingers and sending them ricocheting down onto the road. A car-horn blared.

John and I helped Donny to his feet.

"Thanks, man," he said, wiping his gashed and bloody face. It was badly swollen from his terrible beatdown. "I almost had that big bastard." He actually laughed through his pain.

I saw him staring at his broken stick. A wistful look softened his face.

"I'll miss you, Lannie," he muttered.

"I've got lots of extra sticks, Donny," I said. "You can have any one you want. Any time."

John didn't look so sympathetic, but at least he'd had the good sense not to say something sarcastic, for a change.

The police were on their way. But before they arrived, I had one last bit of business.

"Excuse me, boys," I said, picking up the megaphone. "Attention, citizens of The Village!" I shouted. The megaphone squealed. "I am *not*, nor have I ever been, a Nazi. I hate fascism and racism and bigotry. Rainbow people, continue to fly your unicorn flag. I salute you! Also, *stop* calling me names! Do not call me Humpty Dumpty! Do not call me Eggie! Do not call me Village Vigilante! I am Norbert Reingruber. Good night." I put the megaphone down. I felt good. Really good.

Somehow, the police got the thug down the ladder. We were all assembled around their cruiser, giving statements. "OK, I think we've got everything we need, for now. Thanks for your help, Spiderman," the officer in charge joked.

"Officer, it's been a tough night. Please call me by my name. Thanks. I really appreciate it." *Woah*. Had I, Norbert Reingruber, actually stood up for myself?

The cops shared a look, at my expense, but I couldn't totally blame them. After all, I was still dressed up as the Steeltown Avenger.

Chapter 30

IT WAS ALMOST MIDNIGHT. For two more hours, I'd sat behind my shop counter as a detective with one of those bushy moustaches—Donny always called them *dusters*—grilled me about everything that had happened since my fateful meeting with The Screw at ComWorld.

The shop seemed to be full of friends and police. Interestingly, I'd noticed a couple of officers browsing. Maybe my customer base was going to expand a little, after all this. Most of the neo-Nazis had gone home after my announcement, but a few unicorn kids had snuck in and were taking advantage of the opportunity to browse my new manga arrivals.

Finally, after what seemed an eternity, the police left the shop. I saw through the smashed glass of my front door that the parking lot and street were finally deserted. The dangling neon "B" swayed in a gentle breeze, as if to say "B is for Bummer".

At least the nastiest dwarf on the planet was now in police custody.

As I taped up the door with cardboard, I looked over at the sub shop across the street. It stayed open later than all the other shops. And, for once, I didn't feel like going over there and buying a sub. Progress.

Suddenly, I felt really heavy. I was deeply frazzled, exhausted.

I'd heard Morag enter through our apartment back door. I was always amazed at how easily sound carried through the thin walls. She'd gone to buy a box of donuts. They have been known to heal people from trauma. I hoped she wouldn't be disappointed if I didn't eat any.

Although Morag and I had much to process, I doubted either of us had the energy for that tonight. Perhaps eating together quietly was a good first step towards recovery.

I thought about Mutti. I felt profound relief knowing Hamilton's finest had finally arrested The Screw, and that Mutti was now officially safe. Maybe not from cancer, but from villains, at least. I promised myself I'd see her first thing in the morning, after a solid breakfast. I would hug her and tell her from the bottom of my heart how she was the best Mutti a son could ever have.

I'd almost finished the temporary fix on the door when a gleaming black limo slid up in front of the shop. *Oh no. What now?* The passenger window rolled down, silky smooth.

Slowly, I opened the door.

Staring out at me was a suave-looking older man, in a sophisticated blue suit and designer glasses with turquoise lenses. He looked like he'd never missed a day at the gym.

He held up a copy of *The Steeltown Avenger* and leaned out.

"It's brilliant, Mr. Reingruber," he said. "Even though you *stole* my Invisiblator idea."

"Huh?" I squeaked.

He nodded solemnly. "I understand brilliance, Norbie. The idea came to me in a flash and I imagine it did for you, too. The only difference is that mine is real, but yours isn't."

"I'm sorry, I—"

"Never mind," he said, shushing me with his hand. "Coincidences happen. Luckily for you, I'm a huge comic book aficionado, so I'm giving you a pass. For now." He gave me a faint smile. "*The Steeltown Avenger,* huh?" He winked at me. "It sounds like a winner, Mr Reingruber. Keep up the good work."

His window rolled up.

And the limo slid out onto the road and was gone.

Chapter 31

MORAG DROPPED A BEAUTIFUL bombshell on my noggin.

We'd showered and were plunked on the sofa, stuffing our faces with donuts, still amped up from the insane night.

She put her hand on my lap and wouldn't look me in the eye. She was definitely freaked out. It made me ache inside. I felt like a vulnerable little boy.

"I'm pregnant, Norbie."

I went into the Twilight Zone, automatically picked up a donut and scarfed it. I felt like the time my slot car transformer zapped me.

A flash of fear crossed Morag's face.

And suddenly, I knew everything would be okay.

I felt my face light up into a big-ass smile, and then I started to blubber.

I pulled her into my arms and we sobbed and hugged. "Don't worry, Morag, we're gonna be okay."

Eventually, we found ourselves making the sweet love.

My world had undergone some huge changes recently, and here it was changing again. I mean *really* changing. Morag's news was a beautiful sucker punch that had me feeling like a kid on Christmas morning. I was going to be a dad! Finally. I couldn't believe it. *Wait till Mutti hears the good news! Hot diggety dog!*

That night had ended on such a beautiful note. Who could have predicted after everything that had happened?

Chapter 32

I'd arrived early at my shop. Already, fifty fans had lined up, desperate for Issue No.1, as they had been doing for days. I sat behind the counter and enjoyed my coffee.

A week after the Battle of the Bowling Alley, my groin had almost healed up from doing the splits. I realized with great clarity that some things in my life had definitely changed. Oddly though, some had stayed exactly the same.

After Karl and I brought Mutti home from the hospital, I'd spent as much time as I could with her when I wasn't managing the shop. I'd made sure to put on the bravest face, even after I'd heard the heart-breaking news that her cancer had spread, far worse than what Dr. Khan had first suspected. Mutti was thrilled about the baby coming, so we all tried to stay positive and "life-focused", as Mutti called it.

Fortunately, Karl stayed with Mutti twenty-four/seven and attended to all her needs, and it was the first time since Dad's death that Mutti had allowed a man to live with her full-time. She'd made a good decision, and I told her as much. I was super grateful for Karl and his glass-half-full attitude, and, of course, his love for Mutti, and I realized that this good-hearted and talented man had a lot to teach me about life.

Remember Donny's pseudonym, Dave Walker? The name he ripped off that real guy we'd known from high school? We found out he's alive, but a bit of a mystery. He lives in a tiny cottage-of-a-house down on Burlington Street, across from Dofasco. Donny found his info online. Donny keeps obsessively driving down there and knocking on Dave's door, but Dave never answers. Walker's neighbours say he only comes out late at night, and they've rarely seen him. All his groceries are delivered and left on his stoop. Donny's convinced he's a modern

Boo Radley. Of course, now he's determined to meet Dave face-to-face someday. Yeah, that'll go well.

All the buds think Donny's just desperate to find someone other than Steven to mythologize. Personally, for Walker's sake, I hope Donny *never* finds him.

After the sheet show, Allison had walked out on Donny—again—and bunkered down in a hotel. She'd taken Stewart with her. Donny was an emotional wreck, literally on his knees every day phoning her, begging for forgiveness, crying, promising this time he'd stay on his mood stabilization medication, no matter how weird it made him feel. I felt sorry for all three of the Loves. Somehow, he'd found a way to prove to her he'd gone back on his meds and she'd forgiven him and she came back home, strings attached. She wasn't a cold-hearted woman, but very few women could have put up with Donny the way she had all these years. Just this past week I'd seen a real difference in him. In fact, only yesterday, during a chat at Horton's, he'd whispered to me that his psychiatrist had given him an official diagnosis. He didn't want to share, yet, but he was really glad, because at least now he knew what was wrong with him. "I know I look like I'm having fun," he said, "but sometimes I'm just scared out of my mind, Norb." Boy, did I ever feel for him when he said that.

Ironically, those fuzzin' YouTube Village Vigilante and Humpty Dumpty videos earned Donny enough ad revenue to pay off his billboard debt.

And he actually took down all my videos, although you can still find them, since *nothing* ever disappears from the World Wide Web. But he replaced them with footage of some other poor idiot who calls himself the Hamilton Hammer. He rides the Barton Street bus and breaks up fistfights between riders. He must have some kind of death wish. Those videos get even more views than mine used to get.

I did give myself a break from Donny but not for a year like Morag had wanted me to. After two days, Morag relented. He was back on his meds and trying really hard. He needed a friend. It was clear he was making amends. He knew Morag loved the movies, so he'd bought her a movie pass for two, and was going to treat us to an extra-large, double-cheese, bacon and mushroom pizza from Aurora Pizzeria on our next D&D night. He definitely knew my weaknesses, especially for awesome pizza. He was definitely on the right track to fixing our friendship!

The police didn't charge Tony for pinning the thug, believing he'd acted in self-defence against a known felon intent on murdering him. However, they had fined him for driving his stock car on a city street. After pictures of the "Italian Stallion" went viral, Tony got a number of offers to race his car at tracks in the area. He was tickled pink. But he did tell us he needed a break from us. "Just a few weeks," he said. "This has all been too much, man, even for someone who's gotten pretty used to crazy. No offence."

John, unlike Tony, had come to hockey on Sunday. But after our game, instead of going for coffee with Donny and me, he went straight to his family's restaurant to help prep the Sunday meal, something he'd never done before. Family was becoming more and more important to him. Donny and I were pretty sure he, like Tony, had needed a break from us—from our crazy—so we'd let him have his space. At the best of times, John was hard to read. These days, I recognized that his sarcasm towards other people was probably also part of a critical inner voice he directed towards himself. I decided to cut John a break. After everything we'd been through, we could *all* use one.

Unexpectedly, I got a short email from none other than Steven Dundee, saying he'd seen me on tv and had admired my bravery. He'd told me to keep up the good work, and signed off "Godspeed, Steven". I laughed to myself. Even though Steven was far away, fighting for good in far-away places, I felt part of his heart would always belong to the Village.

After Sifu Po had handed The Screw over to the police, he'd vanished from the scene. I got a postcard from him. He and his wife were on some disco cruise in the Caribbean. He said KC and the Sunshine Band were there. He was pretty stoked. I wrote him a letter of thanks, one I should have written years ago. I imagined his face when he got home and read it. It made me feel good.

Tye Novak is ecstatic. Since its release, *The Steeltown Avenger Issue No. 1* has earned me twenty grand and Tye twice that. Those out-of-the-gate earnings are unprecedented in the comic book business. Easily a down payment on a family home in the Village! I've been keeping the store open seven days a week. Tank and Harlan got a raise, and Morag helps out on the weekend.

Currently, I'm doing an online management workshop run by the City of Hamilton, one Morag paid for, and I'm learning cool stuff I never knew existed, like the dos and don'ts of discipline, workplace harassment, and Ontario labour laws. Although I find it empowering, it's also a little dry and anxiety-inducing. However, for Morag's sake, I'm trying really hard to understand it all. Yesterday, I handed Tank and Harlan a Vacation and Absence Form. I told them future vacations and absence requests must be submitted two weeks in writing prior to the requested time off, and, due to operational needs, may not necessarily be granted. I also told Harlan to act *nicer*—no more toxic work environment. And he finally agreed to add in the online shopping cart feature, realizing that online sales would help keep the business afloat.

I've been working on Issue No. 2 of *The Steeltown Avenger.* Let's just say that it's going to be *totally* awesome. And there is not one single Invisiblator in the whole fuzzin' thing.

I thank God for Morag, for our baby growing inside her, and the hope of new life and love ahead. I'm actually enjoying the process of change. It's scary. It's amazing. It's life.

Would you please leave a review?

DID YOU ENJOY *Norbie Gets Screwed?* If so, would you be kind enough to leave a review, either with the retailer where you purchased this book or at Goodreads? Thank you!

Indie authors rely on the kind reviews of readers to get the word out to others.

Don't miss out!

Visit the website below and you can sign up to receive emails whenever Dave Walker publishes a new book. There's no charge and no obligation.

https://books2read.com/r/B-A-CGLW-JCJEC

BOOKS 2 READ

Connecting independent readers to independent writers.

About the Author

Dave lives with his writer wife, Anne L. Darling, in Hamilton, Ontario, Canada. The author may be reached at: davewalkerauthor@yahoo.com Read more at www.davewalkerauthor.com.